MW01716709

D. LARAY

I Said I Was Gone

Laray D

First published by D. Laray 2023

First edition

ISBN: 979-8-9891442-0-4

This book was professionally typeset on Reedsy.
Find out more at reedsy.com

Dedicated to those who are currently battling abuse.
In honor of victims who have survived domestic violence.
In tribute to the thousands of lives lost every year at the hands of an abuser.

Prologue

Three months ago

The call connects. Sasha's voice is on the other line, confirming her number has yet to change over the last five agonizing years.

"Vivian! I thought I would never hear from you again. How is everything? Please tell me you want your job back."

"No, not quite. Not at all, actually." The sound of her voice is comforting. Uncontrollable words of relief whisper out of me, spilling like red wine on a white carpet. "You said I could always reach out if I ever needed anything." I clear my throat, nervous to continue. "I know we haven't spoken in a while, but-"

Sasha cuts me short with a response of commitment. "And I meant what I said. What is it, Vivian?"

"It's gotten worse," I speak loud enough for her to hear but quiet enough so Ezra can't. "I never thought I would say this, but I'm starting to wonder if I'll make it out of this relationship alive."

Sasha lets out a sigh of disappointment. She predicted the outcome of my relationship with Ezra from the very beginning. "I wish you would have listened to me."

"Me too," I admit, "but I need to make this call quick."

Sasha's voice remains still in contrast to my hurried tone. "You're more than welcome to stay with me. I have a guest room and a second bathroom. My apartment is pet friendly, too." She backpedals on her last statement as if she regrets considering my cat. "Nina doesn't urinate and shit herself in aimless directions, does she?"

"What? No." I shake my head, balking at her question. "Besides, I appreciate the offer, but I can't involve you in this any more than I'm already asking. He will go to any and every measure to make me suffer. Even if that means putting the people closest to me through hell." I say this as if I have people close to me at all. If I did, I wouldn't be calling a former boss to help me escape.

Sasha dismisses my fear with a laugh as if Ezra is her last worry. "Have you decided where you're going to go then?"

"Yes. Back to Chicago," I tell her decisively.

"Vivian, be serious. That's where you're from. You don't think that would be his first guess of where you went?"

"Of course it would, but Chicago is the only place outside of Colorado I know well enough to start over."

"I guess so," she agrees with doubt. "How soon do you want to leave?"

"Six months. *Max.* I will reach out to you when I'm ready. I know you'll be worried sick about me in the meantime, but not a single red flag can be raised. So, please. Do not call me."

"Of course I'll be worried! Are you out of your mind? Six months is way too long. Why wait?"

"I need time to prepare. I don't have the means to pick up and leave this quickly. Disappearing out of nowhere is already stressful enough to attempt, let alone doing it completely broke."

Sasha pauses long enough to make me think we lost connection. Her response is calculated and strategic. "You're right.

Don't be impulsive. I'm going to tell you exactly what you need to do, so listen closely."

Chapter 1

Coming home after a day of surgeries to an immaculately clean home and the smell of dinner are among Ezra's expectations.

At this point, his expectations are more so stipulations. Tonight is no different.

Besides one thing. He's late.

Not knowing where he is or when he'll be home stresses me out. I fidget around, lighting a vanilla bean candle, refolding throw blankets, and fluffing decorative pillows on the sofa. I'm officially unable to find anything more to tidy. The house is already immaculate just the way Ezra likes it.

It's nearly eight o'clock in the evening – hours past when he usually gets home from work. Even though I shouldn't be concerned, given every nefarious thing he puts me through, I can't help it. My mind spins on a hamster wheel, thinking of his whereabouts.

Anxiety accumulates inside me for the worst reasons. A car accident. A mishap in surgery. Cheating. At that thought, and after a dozen calls to his cell phone, I decide to try his business line.

"You've reached the practice of Dr. Ezra Bozzelli. If you get this message, I'm performing surgery, attending a meeting, or out of the office. For urgent matters, dial 911. Otherwise, please leave a detailed message. I or my assistant, Claire Bluff, will contact you shortly. Thank you, and have a great day!"

Claire's name makes my blood boil, but it erupts at him not answering. Worry intoxicates me. Although he always told me to call Claire only in the case of true emergencies, I use my best judgment to deem his coming home late as exactly that.

An emergency.

The line rings numerous times before Claire finally picks up. I pull the phone away from my ear at the sound of loud rummaging in the back as if she were unprepared to answer.

"Hello, this is Claire?" She answers with skepticism.

"Claire, it's Vivian. Ezra's wife."

"Vivian! Of course. H-how have you been?" Her voice always has a fake niceness that gets under my skin.

"I've been better. Ezra still hasn't made it home from work. I was hoping you could tell me when he left the office today." She falls silent, making me impatient after several seconds of no response. "Claire? Are you there?"

"Um, yes. I'm trying to think. I believe he left around his usual time."

"And what time would that have been? I need to know." My patience with her is spreading thin.

"Five o'clock?"

Something about her is off-putting. "You seem uncertain."

"I'm sorry. I just. . ." she sighs with stress. "I don't have a clear answer. It has been a long day for us both. Maybe he is taking a load off. I'm sure everything is alright!"

"Thanks anyway," I say, wondering what kind of load he may be taking off and if he's taking it off with her.

I toss my phone onto the counter next to where a chuck roast simmers on low. The roast emits an aroma that's beginning to make me feel sick after all these hours of waiting. Or maybe it's the thought of the possibilities between Claire and Ezra after years of an established, overly friendly partnership.

I've always wondered if her husband has the same intuition about them as I do. The sick feeling inside me intensifies.

I sprint to the bathroom, tripping over Nina along the way. I barely reach the toilet before I vomit. My curls fall to the front of my face as Nina's fur gropes over my shins. She swivels around my feet and through my legs, meowing with concern.

I attempt to comfort her once I'm relieved, but the sound of the toilet flushing sends her scurrying out of the bathroom.

Before flicking the light off, I'm tempted to reach under the cabinet and grab the box that I've had hidden there for weeks now. I'm not ready.

Instead of dealing with the inevitable, I plop on the couch and stare aimlessly, thinking of where Ezra is. Nina jumps into my lap, somehow sensing that I need her comfort. Our bond is telepathic. She purrs with each of my strokes along her black and gray tattered coat while I continue to worry.

After a few minutes of losing myself in my thoughts again, Nina's ears perk up. Her eyes flutter open at the sound of car tires crumbling across the gravel and the garage door rumbling.

We never know what is on the other side of that door until it opens. She bolts into a corner of the living room and hides.

I approach Ezra with a mix of relief and angst. "Hi, honey. Where have you been?"

Chapter 2

I land on the floor, catching myself at my wrists, but quickly bring them up to shield my face as he stands over me.

"Why did you call Claire? I told you that you should never call my assistant unless it's absolutely necessary!"

"I thought it was! You always let me know when you'll be home. I was worried."

"See, that's your problem. You're psychotic and insecure. You always accuse me of doing something wrong!"

Ezra steps closer to me. I scoot back. Nina meows from a distance. She knows where this is heading.

"All I'm asking is where you've been. I'm not accusing you of anything. I deserve to know. I'm your wife!"

He kneels until we are eye-to-eye. His mouth meets the side of my face as he grabs me by the neck, his favorite placement. Spit lands on my cheek as he speaks.

"I would've told you where I was if you didn't act like a bitch when I walked through the door. Stop trying to control me. It'll never work out for you." He grips tighter. "You should know that by now."

I stare into his malevolent eyes, surrounded by his jungle-like eyelashes. I refrain from saying another word. The situation has already escalated enough. He releases his grip in silence and steps away from me.

As Ezra walks upstairs in his scrubs, I think about how his patients have no idea what type of man cuts into them.

I have an impulse to go after him and put a knife through his back — then again and again. Another part of me knows I have the rest of my life to lose. I hold my composure and go into the kitchen to get dinner ready instead of reaching for a weapon.

I will be out of here soon, I tell myself.

Someone may wonder how I got into this situation in the first place. What they don't know is how easily it happened. I doubted myself, failing to believe the red flags were any sign of what is now my reality.

I wish I could go back and see through the kindness, beyond the charm, and past his appeal. I would've known he was far from benign, tainting every crevice of my life with his demons.

I glance through the window above the kitchen sink as I finish preparing dinner. I make eye contact with our neighbor, Ms. Joyce. She's one of those neighbors who watches everyone and everything. I give her a faint smile, but she walks away shaking her head, not in disappointment or shame, but in sympathy.

I have a feeling Ms. Joyce knows what happens inside these walls. I'm certain she is the one who called the police when it got very violent one night a while back. Unfortunately, law enforcement did nothing but make it worse.

Because Ezra is one of the most renowned plastic surgeons in the country, and women from all around fly for his expertise, no one, not even the police, would believe me anyway.

Filing police reports, depending on loved ones (which is inconceivable when you are in isolation), and other logical ways to get out are not always easy to execute. Ezra got more strategic, bruising me in places easier to cover. He became more calculated at confining me, keeping me tethered to the house.

"Smells good in here."

My shoulders jolt up in fear, and I turn around. I'm met with the sight of Ezra in the pajamas I laid out for him as I do every night. I realize he doesn't deserve it, but it's another way I avoid conflict. It's more for myself than for him.

I ignore his compliment and meet him at the table to serve him the dinner I should have poisoned.

"So, are we going to be mad at each other all night?" Ezra says as if he forgot what he just did to me.

Picking at my food with distaste, I respond with silence. The smell of the roast is getting to me again. I hold my breath as my mouth salivates. I swallow the urge to vomit for the second time tonight.

"Vivian, you know I hate myself for treating you that way. I just wish you would trust me. I love y. . ." And the rest of his words absorb into the air like nothing to me. I have heard all his platitudes before.

Typical Ezra, penetrating me with his screwed version of love. It started as roses full of remorse, a brand-new car of bribery, and a diamond ring with stale promises. What I find is that nothing material can ever hold the apologetic value that actions can.

Ezra scrapes the last bit of roast from his bowl and excuses himself from the table. He leaves me alone to finish my dinner, which I have barely touched.

Before walking away, he turns to me with an expression of epiphany. "Oh, by the way, Claire has been going to a cycle class studio. Since you want to talk to her so badly, maybe you should ask about signing up. I'm sure they have a discount for referrals or something like that. You seem a few pounds heavier lately." Ezra steps away, leaving his bowl for me to clean after him. "I'm going to bed, and you should too, instead of eating the rest of that."

A lump forms in my throat. Tears of rage build up in my eyes, but I fight them before they roll down my face. I don't let him see me cry anymore. I've learned that only fuels him. It gives him power.

I return to the bathroom once he is out of sight and back up the stairs. The sensation of vomit has yet to subside. Nina telepathically finds her way to me once again as I heave over the toilet.

"I know I said you've gained some weight, but I didn't mean you should go bulimic!" Rather than checking to see if I'm okay, he yells sardonically from upstairs. I'm not surprised, though. In fact, I'm thankful.

The water runs to drown out the noise. The door is shut so that Nina doesn't flee when I flush this time. She's like my unregistered support animal after everything she's been around for in my life.

Picking her up in the alley as a stray kitten in high school and hiding her from my mom was easy, considering I was her last priority. Men came first, so she didn't notice for quite some time.

When I moved out of Chicago, I took Nina with me. She's been by my side over the last decade of events in Denver. Now, she is here to undergo this moment alongside me as well.

Deciding I can't wait any longer, I search for the box I hid in the cabinet below the sink. I reach past cleaning supplies and extra tissue rolls.

I begin to feel uneasy as I feel around for it. My movements become frenetic. I try to calm my nerves and remove everything from the cabinet quietly.

It has to be here.

I try assuring myself that if Ezra found it, he wouldn't have waited a single moment to use it against me. At the same time, I remember how spiteful he is. He would wait until just the right moment to shove this in my face. Something I tried meticulously to hide from him.

Faith resurfaces when I notice the corner of it sticking out between supplies. I place everything back in the cabinet quietly, except the box.

The box to a pregnancy test.

The faucet continues to run as I delicately tear the package open. I have been contemplating taking this for weeks now. I've deluded myself into thinking that the possibility was entirely impossible. But Ezra noticing my weight gain was a confirming observation.

If I'm pregnant with his child, I can't afford to hide from the inevitable, nor can I spare the risk of him knowing. He would make sure I never find a way out.

Chapter 3

The pregnancy test directions help me navigate through the process. My hands tremble, making it difficult to do so without making a mess.

I lower myself onto the bathroom floor. My back is propped against the wall for the next three minutes while I wait for the results. My heart races, each beat chasing after the next. Nina's purrs fall in sync as she bundles into my lap.

My eyes flutter closed. Reels of what motherhood would look like ruminate in my mind, the financial aspect of it specifically.

My mom's attempt at motherhood gave me an arduous and poverty-stricken perception. Milk with no cereal. Peanut butter but no jelly. I was given no choice but to smuggle food into my backpack from the school cafeteria.

She worked hard to make the least amount of money possible in order to stay on government assistance. Harder than she did to care for me in basic ways, like teaching me how to insert a tampon or shave my legs in the right direction.

Every month, she sold our food stamps to someone in the neighborhood for half the price. Instead of filling the fridge or replacing my high-water jeans, the proceeds were used to get her nails done or buy something for whatever man she was dating at the time. That seemed to change weekly. Sometimes daily.

Parenting with Ezra would be refreshing in that sense. Our children would be raised in an above-average social class – sheltered from famine and dysfunction with a walk-in pantry of endless snacks.

While each of those upbringings would be on the opposite ends of the spectrum, they would have one thing in common. Noxious men.

My mom used to make herself look like *Mother of the Year* to the random multiples of them that she dated. She bragged about how smart of a daughter she had. What I wish she would've admitted was *why*.

She would twist the lock on the outside of my bedroom door. I was forced to remain there for hours while she pleased men like they were kings as they broke her down like glass with a hammer.

Sometimes, I wonder if what I've accepted in my relationship with Ezra is a direct reflection of what my mother exposed me to.

When she found out I had taken in a stray cat, she hated the idea of having an animal in her house. She eventually came to terms with it after realizing Nina was keeping me company while she was too busy neglecting me.

That may have been the best thing she ever did for me.

Outside of caring for Nina, I consumed myself with homework and countless books from my school library. As soon as I turned sixteen, I found another way to spend my time by getting a job at a restaurant as a server.

All it took was one time for me to slip up with my tips, and my money went missing. Between my mom and the men she let into our house, I could never be too careful. From that point forward, I slept with my cash slipped inside my pillowcase. I never forgot to do so much as to shower without my money being within arm's reach.

From time to time, my high school sweetheart, or nightmare rather, James Pierce, held onto some of the cash for me. He was the only one aware of how my life *really* was outside of school. His father, Mr. Sterling, invited me into their home whenever I needed it, and James came to understand me like no one else could because of that.

The nightmare started when James graduated high school a year before me and moved to New York for a full-ride law program. My in-love teenage self couldn't understand how anything was more important than our relationship. I was left to heal from that, along with everything else.

By the time I graduated high school, I had enough savings to buy a car in cash. I only had myself to thank for that accomplishment. Not wanting my mother to take the credit, I packed up the very few things I had and drove myself to Colorado for a full-ride scholarship. That was when I understood how James could leave the way he did.

One of the most ironic times of my life was arriving at my dorm with sobbing students and their parents surrounding me while I rejoiced in a clean slate in life.

After years of normalcy and upon successfully graduating with a degree in Political Science, I quickly realized that continuing to bartend and serve at restaurants with uncapped tips would earn me more than any entry-level job I could get. Even with my degree.

That was when Ezra swooned into my life as a regular at the bar I worked at. I was a perfect target for him. I was in a constant survival mode, and he identified that immediately. He swept me off my feet as devious as a leopard and as venomous as a mamba.

I like to think his disrespect was non-existent in the beginning. Having been with him for five years now, I have to admit I was naive and overlooked it.

Maybe the fact that he was forty-five with no successful relationships should have warned me. Or maybe that he constantly reminded me about the boob job I needed should have been an indicator. But what did I expect from a plastic surgeon who perfects bodies for a living?

He put on a romantic, gentlemen-driven charade. He could fool anyone. Besides my manager at the bar, Sasha. She caught wind of who he was at his core despite his efforts.

There is something cavalier and stone-cold about him. It's like blood doesn't run through his veins, she would say.

Her first red flag stemmed from the fact that Ezra preferred to be called Dr. Bozzelli in place of his first name. I simply considered that to be his satirical humor.

Sasha's concern solidified one night in particular when Ezra came into the bar with a vase of roses for me. His gesture ended up shattered across the floor when he saw me speaking to another man. Although he was only a customer, it appeared to be dramatically more to Ezra.

He claimed to have accidentally dropped the vase, even purchasing more flowers for me later that day. Sasha didn't buy it. It was demanded and upheld that Ezra was no longer allowed there again.

After that, we married quickly, and his expectations were made even quicker. I fought against my nature of independence but evidently caved into the trap he had set out for me.

He expected me to quit the bar. What he envisioned for his marriage was a woman who wanted to take care of the home.

It took me a while to acquaint myself with that lifestyle. I had to imagine myself having the luxury of spending quality, limitless time with my future children, giving them the attention, affection, and treatment I had the void of in my childhood.

When I quit, Sasha was terrified for me. She told me to keep her contact information somewhere hidden in case I lost it and needed her. I had yet to experience what she accurately predicted.

I tried to placate Sasha by enlightening her about what was in it for me. A life I would've never been able to fathom before. Lavish trips, designer clothes, a big house, nice cars, and the freedom to indulge in the things I love most. So I thought.

After a few months of marriage, everything halted at having freedom when Ezra gradually lured me into isolation. His behavior became volatile, choleric, and controlling. His insecurities seeped through the cracks of his charade. He started tracking my whereabouts at all times, limiting the time I spent with others, and dictating my wardrobe.

Someone might wonder why I would stay in this situation. They'd probably narrow it down to weakness because *why else?* But that's a question they should be glad they don't have to comprehend the answer to.

Ezra's abusive nature was impossibly apparent until our minor disagreements led to reviling arguments. That eventually progressed to physical violence, which also made a gradual appearance.

It started with him raising his voice, then pushing and grabbing. That made its way into choking and marking areas of my body that were easy to hide. In every stage, he has promised he would change his ways. He promised to make it up to me in every way under the sun. I lost myself in those words, believing he would return to the person I thought he was before he showed his true colors. By the time I realized it, leaving was easier said than done.

Not only is this a lonely position to be in, but dangerous. Ezra would go to great lengths to keep me from making a break from his shackles. He promised those lengths could end my life, and while he rarely keeps a promise, that's something I can't put past him.

I have to survive in every sense of the word. As much as I crave a household with a father figure, the desperation to have a nuclear family does not run deep enough for me to raise a child in an environment of fighting, belittlement, and cruelty.

At that, I run out of recollections and hypotheticals to pass the time. I'm sure the three minutes the pregnancy test directions told me to wait have been up for a while now.

I stand to my feet, Nina following suit with a whine. My chest fills with a gulp of air, and I hesitate to turn the test over to the resulting side.

After a few more wasted seconds, I impetuously flip it over as if ripping off a band-aid. I push myself away from the counter, flapping both hands over my mouth that hangs open. My heart palpitates at a positive result. I immediately kick myself for only getting one test. Why the hell would I get ONE?

Now I see why women take multiple of them because this feels unreal.

I look at myself in the mirror through a blurry line of teary vision when his strident yell travels from upstairs. "Vivian! What are you doing in there?"

Aggressive footsteps follow his voice down the stairs, and

Nina coils into a corner of the bathroom.

My heart runs a marathon with the scarce time I have to hide my secret from him that noticeably lies on the counter.

His anger burgeons when the doorknob struggles against his force to turn with the lock that's latched into place. He chuckles evilly with a threat. "You know how this goes, Vivian. I'm giving you five seconds to unlock this door."

I spin in circles with terror, trying to figure out what to do with the pregnancy test and its packaging.

"One. . ."

The garbage is too obvious. Flushing it down the toilet is impossible.

"Two. . ."

My hands lay over my chest at the exhaust of my options.

"Three. . ."

My body goes stiff at my final resolution before sprinting into action.

"Four. . .Five."

Chapter 4

The weight of Ezra's body charges into the bathroom after several attempts. Shards of wood from the door frame fly in every direction.

His eyes are stone-cold and filled with nothing. They dart around, trying to piece together what I was doing. I can tell he's losing his patience as he paces back and forth. Ezra dumps the trash can upside down and peeks under the cabinet. He yanks the shower curtain back but finds nothing.

Without any luck, Ezra begins to rage.

His rough hand grips my neck and shoves me with a force strong enough to cause me to tumble into the shower. An instant headache plagues me.

Nina challenges him with hisses, but his kick to her abdomen sends her out of the bathroom screeching. My gut wrenches for her.

"Tell me what you were doing. NOW!"

"I didn't feel well. That's all," but we both know that's a lie.

His breaths are shallow and quick. His fists curl into balls. "Where's your phone?"

My eyes travel to where it lies on the counter. He picks it up and leaves me behind. If the door weren't broken, he would probably have found a way to lock me in the bathroom.

"You aren't getting this back until you tell me what you were doing in here," he yells down to me as his steps travel back up the stairs.

I bring myself back to the moments before he barged into the bathroom.

I envy the women who are dramatically excited at a positive result. They plan a mystery surprise to tell their husband. They slowly share the news with their family and friends who are ecstatic for them. Love lingers through the air for months through gender reveals, baby showers, and diaper parties.

Meanwhile, devastation rather than excitement monopolizes my entire being.

I'm standing in a bathroom with a door broken by an irreverent man who I suspect of cheating with his assistant. Not to mention, I have a positive pregnancy test hidden in the back of the toilet tank. I decide to leave it there because if he didn't think to look there in the first place, hopefully, he never will.

I might be foolish in many ways, staying with Ezra being one of them, but I have to give myself credit where it's due. From hiding my money from my mom because I knew she would steal it to now trapping a covert pregnancy test in a toilet tank, I must say I'm an impressive smuggler.

I could also consider the time I hid Sasha's number and email she wrote down for me when I quit my job at the bar. I slipped the piece of paper into the bible on my bookshelf. That was a place I knew Ezra would never look. Hell would have to rise, turning the sky into a blanket of blazing flames, the ground into boiling lava, and rain into sizzling ash before he would consider opening a bible.

Fear almost prevented me from keeping Sasha's information,

but had I let that happen, the wheels of my escape wouldn't be turning as they are.

Three months ago, when I reached a breaking point and felt courageous, I delved into the bible and located the piece of paper that Sasha scribbled onto at the bar years ago.

I should have called her sooner, but I knew I could not afford to cry wolf with the one person willing and able to help me leave. I knew that if I ever reached out, I needed her to take me seriously. I needed to be ready.

Having been several years, I knew there was a strong possibility her number could've changed since then. Her email could be dormant or one she no longer checks.

I fabricated many other anxiety-driven assumptions, one being if Sasha was in cahoots with Ezra all along and planned to report back to him.

I burdened myself with endless *what-ifs.* Eventually, I figured that whatever the outcome would be, it could not be any worse than my current situation.

One possibility I didn't consider was not having a phone to make the final call to Sasha, letting her know I'm ready.

Although I planned to leave regardless, I'm determined to find my way out of this situation sooner than expected. Not for me, but for my baby. With or without a phone. By any means.

Chapter 5

Last night was a turning point for me. My intuition that I'm pregnant was confirmed, and Ezra noticed my weight gain, coming too close to finding out why.

If I'm going to get out of this relationship, I need to make it happen soon, so this morning, I left home not long after Ezra went to work.

My windshield wipers move at full speed, fighting against pellets of incessant raindrops. Through difficult visibility, I arrive at the bar and drive to the back alley. I snuggle into a space surrounded by overgrown bushes and trees. A dangling branch infested with leaves hugs my car, making me feel secluded.

Before getting too comfortable, I observe from afar to see if I notice cameras that may have been installed since I quit. With none that I can tell, I plan to stick around until Sasha takes a smoke break or takes the trash out. She rarely has a day off, so I know she's here. She has to be.

If there's one thing about someone addicted to cigarettes, they will smoke no matter the weather conditions, unless they're anything like my mother. That woman masked the walls of our home with gunk instead of taking her habit outdoors.

This makes me confident that Sasha will make her way into

the alley at some point. I know she cannot go an entire shift without a puff. My only hope is that she does before 5:00 p.m., giving me enough time to get home before Ezra does.

I already have dinner in the crockpot, the house is spotless, and his change of clothes is prepared for his arrival just as he expects. That leaves me many hours ahead, so I shut the car off to preserve my gas.

Tension builds as I wait for Sasha to turn up. I hope she does. Soon.

The thought of Ezra tracking me down by my location forms a knot that seems to tether around every organ. I instinctively search for my phone to turn it off. The acrobatic feeling in my stomach continues until I remember he took it last night and never gave it back. I feel like a fool.

My head falls back to the headrest, and I let out a sigh of relief that was held in the depths of my lungs. My heart rate dwindles to a livable speed, and my stomach untangles. I feel able to breathe again.

This was another one of those times my mind plays tricks on me because of what Ezra puts me through.

Sometimes, my imagination fabricates his voice yelling out my name and shooting orders at me like a machine gun. His footsteps approach me in public while I'm alone. My ears make up other sounds that aren't there, such as my phone ringing, because God forbid I don't answer his calls on the first ring.

These things happen especially after days like yesterday of broken doors, holes punched into the walls, and bruises left behind.

My anxiety hits an all-time high, but now I have more than myself to fight for.

As the rainfall rushes, my eyes are glued to the back door of the building when it swings open, and a body slips out. My chest squeezes with excitement. I sit up straighter, hoping to see Sasha.

I spot a cook I recognize instead, so I sink back into my seat, a bit farther this time.

Although it feels like it has been at least an hour, I check the time, and only twenty minutes have passed. I undo my seat belt buckle and cross my legs, accepting that I'll be here for a while.

I crack open the book I brought to keep me occupied. I glance up from it periodically at the motion I catch in my peripheral, none of it being that of Sasha.

Yet.

Chapter 6

The morning sickness lasts all day, so I'm not sure why it's called that. Outside of the one time I had to get out of the car to vomit, I have cooped myself inside.

The time is now 4:37 p.m. It's well into the last half hour that I can afford to continue camping out here.

My pessimistic thoughts are interrupted when the back door of the bar opens again. At this point, I have stopped getting my hopes up because I am disappointed time and time again when it's not Sasha that I see.

To my surprise, my eyes widen with thrill when they snag onto her half-shaved head. I drop my book. It flops to the floor, losing the page I left off on. My hand grips the door handle, but just as I open it, someone follows behind her. She isn't alone.

I drown back in my seat but not too far. My gaze is split between the time on the clock and the two of them as they shield themselves from the rain under a covered part of the building. They spark their cigarettes together for a smoke break. Now, I am left to hope she notices me somehow.

My first time meeting Sasha was at my interview years ago, where I was hired on the spot after the first few questions. She shared that there was something about me that reminded her of herself. She recognized a peculiarity and resonated with it right off the bat. I always wondered what that meant.

It gave me hope that if she was cut from a similar cloth with a past as rough as mine, maybe I could be as eclectic and radiant as her one day, the type of woman who intimidates quietly and inspires without trying.

Sasha always carried herself mysteriously, yet ironically had an open-book way about her. She would share enough information about herself to where you *think* you knew her through and through, but the real her was as deep as the ocean floor.

As I continue to observe, I think maybe it's optimism or delusion, but I could swear I notice Sasha's eyes discreetly peeping at me between her cigarette puffs.

In the thick of my thoughts, I debate taking my chances and walking up to the two of them, but I need to be level-headed. The last thing I need is someone to rumor that I met with Sasha right before leaving my husband and escaping to another state.

I glance back down at the clock. It now reads 4:45 p.m.

They pat their cigarettes out on the ground and go back inside. The door slams closed behind Sasha. It feels like every ounce of hope I had just left with her.

Even if I wanted to take my chances, the one I had was now gone.

Tears sting through as my forehead leans onto the steering wheel at a loss, and self-pity consumes me, but not for long, considering the time.

My car jerks over potholes in the alley as I pull away, forcing me to exit at an awfully slow speed. I feel pathetic having come here so optimistically.

My mood shifts from defeat to delight when the rear-view

mirror reflects movement trailing from a distance. It's Sasha. My foot strikes the brake pedal.

My car doesn't move another inch as she jogs the rest of the way to the passenger side. The door swings open, and she hops in out of breath. Her hair is soaked and plastered over her forehead from the rain that has yet to stop since this morning.

"Vivian!" Her arms reach over the middle console and cling around me. The scent of cigarette smoke and fresh rain fills the air. "Is everything okay?" She frees me of her hug and lays her hands on each of my shoulders, analyzing my face. "I'm going to guess *not* since you've been sitting in the back alley of the bar for God knows how long." Her head cocks to one side as she hones in on my neck. "What the hell did he do to you? Why didn't you call me?"

I lay my curls over my chest as if it would erase what she saw from her memory. "I don't know what I was going to do if you didn't notice me. He has my phone."

I look at the time, and it's now 4:50 p.m. "Listen, I will tell you everything, but right now, I need us to focus on finding a way out before I'm stuck. I know I told you I needed six months, but I need to leave much sooner."

Chapter 7

"How far along are you? Does Ezra know?"

My palm faces Sasha as I hold my hand out, gesturing for her to stop firing questions. "I only found out last night. I have suspected it for a while now, but to answer your question, no. Ezra doesn't know, but he mentioned I've put on weight."

"What an asshole," Sasha says as her thumbs rapidly move across her cell phone screen.

Feeling ignored, I tap her shoulder. "Sasha, I didn't come here to vent. I'm here because I need you. I thought you would understand that. I need to make it back home before he does."

She turns the screen of her phone to face me. "A red-eye flight to Chicago departs at 12:30 a.m."

"Tonight?!"

"*Yes,* tonight! As much as I would love for you to stay, that would be selfish of me. The longer you wait this out, the longer you keep yourself and your baby in a dangerous situation."

After staring at the screen to review the details of the flight she shined at me, I titter at her optimism that I'd be able to afford it.

"I don't have eight hundred dollars for a plane ticket on top of finding a hotel, eating for two, and everything else I probably haven't thought of." I sit back in my seat, feeling defeated. Again.

Sasha's face contorts as she thinks through my options. "What if you stayed with your mom for a little while? Find a job nearby. Make some sacrifices to save up, and then move in time to have your baby." She shrugs as if this is a good idea. "Maybe you two could rekindle and make up for lost time."

I'm disgusted that she would even think I'd be willing to escape my current situation only to go back to the one that landed me here in the first place.

"Are you out of your mind? It has been nearly a decade, and that woman hasn't tried locating or contacting me. I did both of us a favor by leaving back then. I'll do whatever it takes to afford a hotel for my peace and sanity."

She holds her hands up in defense. "Okay! I get it. I'm sorry I even mentioned it. But you should have enough money for a flight if you stuck to the plan. Did you do what I told you to do?"

When we spoke a few months back, Sasha advised me to make excessive trips to the grocery store, pay inside for gas, and make as many pit stops that wouldn't seem out of the ordinary as possible.

The purpose was to request the highest possible cash back at checkout each time, which Ezra's credit card sponsored. The amounts were relatively small enough to barely reflect a dint in his surgeon-funded bank account.

I had to stash the cash away, which was the easy part. I'm realizing using it to escape is the hard part.

"Of course I stuck to the plan. Whenever I got the chance. It was a genius idea you had, but I only have about two thousand dollars."

"I'll take care of it."

My eyes squint at Sasha, trying to understand her correctly. "You mean you're going to buy my plane ticket?"

"That's exactly what I mean," Sasha confirms with certainty.

I can tell it'll be hard to talk her out of this, but I try. "You know I can't let you do that. Plus, Nina is coming with me. I would never leave her with him."

"I know how important she is to you. We'll make it work. Just accept the offer, Vivian. How bad does it have to get for you to finally say you've had enough? He has done the worst of the worst. It seems like the only thing he hasn't done is cheat on you!"

I give her a telling stare.

"You cannot be serious."

"Relax, I don't know for sure!" I try to placate her, but I know it's too late. "He came home way later than usual last night. I called Claire, his assistant, to see if she knew when he left work. Maybe I'm overthinking it, but it seemed she was hiding something from me, and he was pissed I called her."

She whips her head over her shoulder. "Is that not the woman that you always told me made you feel. . . off?"

I confirm with a nod. Sasha knew of my thoughts about Claire Bluff from the start. Claire was the one person I could tell Ezra had a *different* type of chemistry with when he introduced me to the employees in his practice at the beginning of our relationship. Something amorous lingered.

"This is rock bottom. Your intuition tells you you're part of a love triangle with a man that breaks you down physically and emotionally. To make matters worse, you're pregnant with his child," she tells me what I already know. "Trust me when I say you need to leave. Tonight."

I look at the clock, and it's 4:56 p.m., leaving us barely any time to spare.

"Alright, fine, but I'm trusting you. We have one shot. This has to work because if it doesn't, and he finds out I tried to leave, he'll make sure I never can."

Sasha grabs my hand and squeezes with determination. "We'll make sure this works out for you. Believe me."

"Book it," I say abruptly because if I don't rip the band-aid off now, I don't know if I ever will.

Sasha's face lights up with excitement. She drops my hand and reaches for her phone. "Okay, so here's the plan. I'll be outside to pick you up around 9:30 p.m., giving you a one-hour window to find your way out of there so you can make the 12:30 a.m. flight on time." She hands the phone over to me with the notepad screen open. "Here, type your address."

I groan at how difficult this is going to be. I'm skeptical of how it will work as smoothly as Sasha thinks. "Do you think it's easy for me to slip away under his nose? And what if someone notices you? In the type of neighborhood we live in, unknown vehicles don't lurk outside without someone noticing and reporting it." As I hand the phone back, I remind her what she's getting herself into.

"I know what I'm doing," she says with credibility.

My chin falls to my chest, and my hand meets my face as I relish what's happening. I run my fingers through my hair with a sigh of stress and try to absorb the magnitude of what is to come. My gut fires up with fear, doubt, and hesitation, and my chest clogs with heaviness.

It's almost as if she sees the concoction of emotions building up inside me. Sasha's arms stretch over, smothering me tightly into a hug identical to the one when she first got into the car.

"Congratulations, Vivian. I know you're scared, and it doesn't seem like it now, but this will be one of the best things to ever happen to you."

Unable to thank her for congratulating me because of how terrible this all feels, I politely push her away until our eyes meet.

"Why have you always cared so much?" It's a genuine question I've always wanted to know.

"Just take the blessing and consider it my gift to you." Sasha looks away from me and opens the door. Her legs swing out of the car, and she stands up to walk back to the bar.

"Wait!" I stop her. "Thank you." I wish I could find better words to express my appreciation.

She leans her head back into the car and smiles softly. "I'm proud of you. I'll see you later." She slams the door closed and jogs back down the alley through the rain.

I realize I stayed too long with a glance down at the clock that reads 5:03 p.m. I shift my car back into drive and resume jolting over potholes. The raindrops fall hard on the windshield as I exit the parking lot and pick up speed.

Thoughts of gratitude consume my drive home. Attempting something this extreme without someone like Sasha is unimaginable.

While I was envious of the women who have loving men, family, and friends by their side throughout pregnancy, I realize there are people in my situation without a way out. Although it feels like I don't have anything to feel grateful for, it could always be worse.

Many others in my position have loved ones who walk away and look down on them, criticizing and inflicting judgment to no end. I find it hard to blame them for their ignorance. It's something they don't understand because no one should have to.

I realize I'm getting ahead of myself with enthusiasm. Just because a plan is mapped out doesn't mean it will work. Especially when I arrive home, and the garage grinds open. My heart freezes like a block of ice when I see Ezra's car parked.

He made it home from work before I did.

Chapter 8

It shouldn't surprise me that Ezra tried to throw me for a loop, making it home not only earlier than he did yesterday but earlier than usual, unfortunately, and conveniently before me.

I pull into the garage and lock the doors to my car as if he wouldn't bust the window out like he did to the bathroom door last night. My skin crawls with paranoia. My head swivels from left to right, looking for a sign of Ezra.

My gut tells me it will be a long night of cat and mouse. This reminds me of the time I left last year in the winter for a few hours to be the bigger person after a night of arguing.

The tension the morning after was as thick as an encyclopedia. It felt as though we were roommates rivaling over someone not paying a portion of their rent. My logic was that we were equally in need of alone time to decompress. I stuffed a book into my purse and went to a nearby coffee shop. I ended up staying long enough to finish the book from front to back and got wired up off of three lattes on his dime.

By the time I left, the bipolar Colorado weather had taken a turn. Several inches of snow rolled its way in. I treaded lightly on the treacherous roads, barely controlling the car as it slipped and slid.

Once I made it home safely, I was ready to work the situation out with Ezra. Of course, to do so, I needed to get into the house, which he made impossible. The codes and locks on every door were changed.

Ezra peered through the living room window facing the driveway. He watched me keep warm in my car while snow accumulated around me as I waited for him to have mercy. That lasted several hours – long enough that my gas tank nearly ran out of fuel, forcing me to cut it off.

Our neighbor, Ms. Joyce, was observing from a distance as she always does. The poor woman trekked through several feet of snow with a blanket. Bundled up in a knitted scarf and a hat she had probably made herself, she approached my driver's side window with a tenuous knock.

The glass of the window fought against ice to roll down, and crisp air wisped snow into my face once it did. That was my first time getting a close look at Ms. Joyce's smooth, nearly wrinkle-free skin, rich with melanin.

"Ms. Joyce, how are you?" But she was not a woman of many words, if any. She handed the blanket to me and walked away, staring directly at Ezra through the window for as long as she could. Her eyes may have been more vicious than his that day.

Ezra eventually let me in, although I went weeks without the new keys or codes to the doors. I had to earn them back by doing everything he asked, from giving demanded massages that he didn't deserve to scrubbing random scuffs on the walls, which were from arguments that turned violent throughout our relationship.

That was incredibly triggering, but it's also why today seems eerily peaceful when I get out of the car with still no sign of him. The unlocked garage door leads me into the front entryway, and the house is completely silent.

Nothing but stillness and the smell of dinner simmering in the crockpot from this morning exists.

I'm instantly more concerned when Nina doesn't come running to bunt against and between my legs, begging for my attention.

I amble down every hall, into each bathroom, up the stairs, and back down the stairs, scoping out every room without a word – bracing myself to see Ezra, and with hopeful anticipation to find Nina.

Ezra's car is here, but he is not. And neither is Nina. They're both gone.

Feeling conquered and outsmarted, I become worried for Nina and fearful of what he's capable of. Defeated thoughts occupy my mind in replace of anxiety.

Why am I even trying? Why leave when I don't have a solid plan in place once I make it to Chicago? Maybe Sasha was right when she expressed her concern about my destination. He'll guess where I'd gone with ease. He's always a few steps ahead of me.

I question if my decision to leave will ultimately give my child the life they deserve when I'm fleeing financial comfort. Not only will I barely have the money to support myself, let alone a child, but he has all the money and resources to support a family *and* the means to find where I disappeared to.

My despaired feelings are interrupted by a delicate knock on the door. My body hardens with a blend of bewilderment and trepidation. For a second, I think I may be hearing things. Maybe my mind is messing with me again. But whoever it is is persistent, as they knock once more – only a bit louder this time.

I peer through the peephole reluctantly and notice not only Ms. Joyce but Nina cradled in her arms.

I unlock the door with haste. "Oh, my God!" She hands Nina over to me, and her coat of fur is completely saturated with rain as if she'd been outside all day. "I was looking everywhere, wondering how she could have gotten out! Thank you so much for bringing her back, Ms. Joyce."

"Oh, she didn't get out on her own. That was no accident." Did I just hear Ms. Joyce's voice for the first time?

My head draws to one side, and my eyebrows furrow as I pet Nina, hoping she doesn't feel like I abandoned her. "I'm sorry. What do you mean by that?" But instead of enlightening me, she returns to her silence with a raise of her eyebrows, giving me a, *you know what I mean,* stare before walking back through the lawn to her house.

She always finds her way over in the worst weather conditions, so the least I can do is watch her until I can see she made it inside safely. I check my surroundings before closing the door and setting Nina on the ground.

Grabbing each side of her wet muzzle as her whiskers tickle my hands, I scratch her by the ears, apologizing profusely, asking her how she got out as if she could respond to me with anything other than purrs and meows.

With Nina in my shadow and Ezra still nowhere to be found, I lead her to her bowl of water and spoil her with a can of soft food. She devours it in seconds.

I've always heard that you can tell a person's level of sanity by how they treat animals. Ezra makes this stereotype ring true.

Anything he can do to hurt me is not off-limits. Anything. He let my cat out, knowing of the feral animals that roam around.

The cars that could have hit her. Knowing she might never make it back.

With that in mind, I scoop her up and go down the steep flight of steps to the basement. I want to make Ezra feel like he is in control. I want him to get wrapped up in his own game so much that he doesn't realize my escape. So I leave Nina in the basement.

I feel like my neglectful mother as I close the door behind me and climb the stairs. I take a second walk through the entire house. Chills travel up my spine with still no sign of him. When he'll finally decide to make an appearance remains beyond me.

What he doesn't realize while he's working against me is that all of this is in my favor. Taking his absence as an opportunity, I prepare for my flight out.

Yesterday, I consumed myself with his whereabouts. But tonight, I have a plan, and it must work. I grab a duffel bag from the closet and head to the dresser to start packing.

I don't make much progress before the bag slips from my stiff, horrified hands. My eyes catch a black metal object protruding from under the pillow on Ezra's side of the bed. In doubt of what I think it is, I walk over and lift it with hesitance.

My fear unlocks. I wheeze at the sight of what sends a zap of terror through me. My heart pumps out of my chest. I have never known Ezra to own a gun or even have the desire to.

Chapter 9

I work myself up with hypothetical scenarios of how Ezra may have planned to use the gun. What would have happened if I didn't find it tonight? What if I wasn't escaping? When did he even get the damn thing?

In a pursuit to protect the life of my child and me from whatever his intentions were, I use one of his shirts to pick it up and hide it somewhere he wouldn't think to look. I carefully carry it down into the kitchen, where I rummage through the cabinets in search of the perfect place to stash. I almost want to keep it for myself, but that's not part of the plan.

I spot a box of a blender. It was a wedding gift we graciously expressed gratitude for but never bothered to open afterward. I drop it inside the box, feeling proud of myself for yet another impressive hiding tactic.

I check the clock on the stove, and it reads 7:00 p.m., under three hours until Sasha should be here.

With still no sign of Ezra, I resume my attempt to pack the duffel bag strategically. Starting with the cash back I've accumulated and hidden into a makeup bag inside my nightstand, I place that at the bottom for everything else to cover.

Thin fabrics of clothes with stretchy, forgivable material,

such as leggings, and oversized clothes, such as T-shirts, are my method of fitting as much as possible. The clothes I'm packing serve a dual purpose, given a belly that will eventually grow too large for anything else.

Taking up the rest of the space is other necessities. My ID, a book, and a personal debit card to an old account I never closed, which Ezra knows nothing about.

My fully packed bag bursts at the seams and through the zippers as I haul it into the laundry room, where I throw it into the drum of the dryer machine. Because he hasn't had the responsibility of using it in years, it's a place he would never think to look. He might not even remember how it works.

Ezra hasn't lifted a finger since well before we moved in together. When we bought this house (well, he did, but he was nice enough to put me on the mortgage), I replaced the housekeepers who washed and folded his underwear and cleaned his dirty dishes.

With Nina and my packed bag tucked away, I plop onto the couch and lay a hand on my pregnant belly. Resting my hand here feels comforting after an incredibly exhausting day. Although I can't determine how far along I am, I know I'm at the awkward stage of whether I am pregnant or just gaining weight. Ezra told me so. I look up at the clock. It's nearly 8:00 p.m. I'm still mind-boggled that his car is here, but he's not.

Sasha should be coming soon if she sticks to the plan. Without a phone to call her and let her know she could come much sooner to get me out of here, I am bound to spend the next hour and a half fighting my sleep and hoping Ezra and I don't cross paths when it's time to leave.

Chapter 10

A car door shutting in the driveway serves as my alarm clock. I'm shaken out of my slumber that I barely remember slipping into. I rub my eyes for clearer vision to read the clock.

I lost my fight to sleep, leaving me five minutes to get outside to Sasha if I want to make it to the airport in time. If I don't get out there to meet her, she will probably think I'm stuck in here or that I've changed my mind.

Climbing over the couch to look to the driveway through the window, I notice a stumbling, inebriated Ezra walking from a silver car that dropped him off.

As it drives away, the headlights illuminate too bright to be able to tell who's driving. I hope they didn't cross paths with Sasha since she should be outside waiting on me by now.

I hear Ezra's keys jingling as he struggles to unlock the door. As much as I want to explode and go ballistic, I quickly lay back down on the couch and pretend to sleep. Arguing with him will only compound the problem and shorten the time crunch I'm already up against.

Where the hell was he, and with whom?

I battle to bite my words when he enters through the door. My eyes struggle to remain closed. By the sounds of him holding himself up on the walls and tripping over his own feet, I can tell he's struggling. He walks directly past me on the couch, and even though I can't see him if I had to guess, he is practically crawling up the stairs. He is belligerent.

All I can hope is that he's too drunk to notice I'm gone in the next five minutes, although I'm almost positive he didn't notice me anyway.

I hear the shower switch on upstairs. The water falls for several seconds before I realize this is my time to go. I push myself off the couch and race against time to the basement for Nina.

She claws at me as I stuff her inside the travel carrier I've had for her since transporting her to move in with Ezra. Feeling terrible, I managed to zip her in.

My legs burn as I climb the steep stairs, the most exercise I've done in a while. With the shower still running, I have high hopes that Ezra cannot hear Nina whining and clawing.

Panting out of breath, I run to the laundry room to retrieve my duffel bag from the dryer machine. On my way to the front door, passing the kitchen, I slip my engagement ring off my finger and place it on the counter beside my purse to ensure he gets the point.

I thread my arm through the loop of my bag and grip my hand around the handle of Nina's carrier just as the shower cuts off. I have no time to contemplate. The front door creaks as I try to open it as slowly and discreetly as possible.

I run instead of walk down the driveway.

Once I make it to the end and look down each side of the street, I notice it's completely vacant. There are no cars, which means the silver one is long gone, an there is no Sasha. I cannot imagine her leaving me behind after the lengths I went to contact her today. Does she think I changed my mind?

Too late to go back inside, I stand in the driveway foolishly, returning to the doubtful question of *why. Why am I even trying?*

A rumbling engine from a distance swallows my thoughts, followed by blinding headlights rounding the corner of the street. Not wanting any neighbors to bust me in the act and potentially expose me to Ezra, I find the nearest bushes to squeeze between and everything else behind them the best I can.

Fear becomes more prevalent as the car drives slower the closer it gets. And then it completely stops in front of me.

Chapter 11

"Vivian," a voice yells softly out the window, "get in here. You're already late enough!"

I look out from the bushes to see Sasha sitting in the driver's seat. It was too dark for me to tell it was her car. I yank Nina and my bag out from the bushes and jog to the passenger side to hop in.

"Sorry! I didn't expect you to take a joyride around the block, so I hid when I saw headlights."

"And I still can't believe you're bringing an entire cat with you," Sasha bickers back.

"Was I supposed to bring half of her? I was serious when I said she's coming with me." I have barely shut my door before Sasha drives off. "Goodness, can I get in first?"

She ignores my complaint as if her erratic driving is normal, "I might hate animals, but I know how much she means to you, so I bought a ticket for her too."

"Oh, my God. I didn't even think about that." Her proactivity allows me to relax. "Thank you for not giving up on me and leaving. I fell asleep on the couch, and if it weren't for Ezra coming home drunk out of his mind, I would probably still be there."

"He was out late *again*?" Sasha asks as she speeds through a stop sign. I forgot how recklessly she drives.

"Yes. His car was home when I returned, but he wasn't. I don't know who he was with, but someone in a silver car dropped him off." I stop and think for a moment before sitting up from my seat with a revelating thought. "Sasha, did you see a silver car while you waited?"

"No, I didn't see any cars at all."

I hoped she had. I wanted to know who dropped my husband off late and intoxicated.

I deflate back into the seat. "He probably went to a happy hour. He's going to sleep as hard as a rock tonight." I fill her in on everything my day comprised, and as I do, I feel even more motivated to leave for good. "When I finally made it outside and didn't see you, I thought you left me."

"I would never, and as a matter of fact, I didn't see that silver car, but I did see a neighbor. That's why I took laps around the block. They were staring into the depths of my soul through their window. Must be the neighborhood watcher."

My gut clenches into a ball. "What neighbor are you talking about?"

"The old lady that lives right next door to you." Sasha looks away from the road and at me. "Don't get me wrong. She looks sweet, but she was freaking me out."

I get a little defensive once I realize who she's talking about. "Oh yes, of course. That's Ms. Joyce. She was the one who brought Nina back over today. She's nothing to worry about. If anything, she looks out for me."

"You can't trust everybody, Vivian." I don't have it in me to argue with her over Ms. Joyce because Sasha could be right; I don't know her intentions. I can't trust her. I shouldn't, anyway.

We get onto the highway, and the rest of the car ride is silent as I take in my surroundings one final time.

Being in Denver for almost a decade was a cross between the best and worst decision I could have ever made. The best because I removed myself from a damaging environment, but the worst for putting myself into yet another one.

Time is a thief; either you're praying for it to speed up to get to the good stuff, or you're wishing for it to slow down to catch your breath. Other times, you wish you had the ability to rewind and change the course of your life.

This has always been a battle of mine; either I was enjoying myself for a split second but dreading my return to reality, or I was in my reality, longing for a change. Right now, I wish I could completely fast forward, skipping everything in between, to a time when life feels worth living.

"Almost there!" Sasha announces loudly, startling me out of my thoughts.

We get off the exit to the airport, and it feels as though caterpillars rebirth inside me. Unhinged butterflies flutter in my stomach. Excitement and doubt fight against each other, making me feel an emotion more intense and complex than I have ever felt in my life. I have felt complex emotions through everything I've experienced, but never this one. I can hardly believe I'm doing this.

Sasha switches to the departure lane of the terminal, making this moment feel all too real. We park in an empty spot on the curb, and she begins tirading me as if I don't know how to travel. "You don't have large bottles of hygiene items, do you?"

"No, no liquids in the bag at all."

"You have your wallet, right?"

"Yes, *mom,*" I answer her sarcastically. Staying at a hotel for the foreseeable future has perks; I don't need to make room for items such as soaps and lotions. "I only brought what I needed. I had no phone to bring, so I left my purse, keys, and even my engagement ring to ensure there's no confusion. I want him to know it was a conscious choice. One he didn't see coming."

"I just want to make sure you're prepared. Once I pull off, there's no turning back. But here…" Sasha reaches into her purse and pulls out a cell phone and charging cord. "I put you on my phone plan. Call me every step of the way. My number is already programmed."

"Oh, Sasha. You didn't have to do this."

"Of course I did. How else am I going to get a hold of you?" She makes a good point. Without a phone, the isolation would be even worse once in Chicago.

My mouth forms a faint smile as I twist the phone in my hands as if I've never seen one in my life. The airport police officer blows his whistle at us. "Keep it moving!"

"Alright, get out and give me a hug," Sasha says as she unbuckles her seat belt.

Feeling rushed into a whirlwind of sudden change, I follow suit with hesitation. My body moves slowly out of the car.

Sasha creeps up behind me, grabs my duffel bag and Nina from the back seat, and holds them out for me to take. "You got this." My lips quiver, and my eyes well with tears. She envelopes her arms around my body and hugs me firmly, squeezing tears out of me. "You better get going. You're cutting it close. Call me when you make it. And remember, my number is the only one saved. You can't miss it."

I simply nod in response. The lump at the base of my throat tells me if I say another word, I'll break down in tears.

Sasha walks around to the other side of her car and gets in.

She rolls down the passenger side window and yells to me before driving away. "Safe travels! You got this!"

Boarding begins in less than thirty minutes, so without enough time to shake myself out of the funk I'm in, I spin around, making my way into the airport that holds my destiny.

Chapter 12

"Passenger Vivian Bozzelli, this is the final call for Flight 3467 to Chicago, Illinois. The gate will close in one minute."

So much for going under the radar.

My name has been called overhead numerous times as my feet gallop across the ground. The last thing I needed.

Bringing Nina aboard was more complicated than I expected. After wasting time arguing with the airline to allow her on the plane with me, I settled with the fact that she would have to be stored in the cargo area at the rear end of the plane.

I make it to the gate in the nick of time. "Miss. Bozzelli?"

Tempted to throw my hand over the attendant's mouth to muffle the sound of my name, I confirm as politely as I can. Everyone has already heard it anyway. "Yes, ma'am."

Carrying his last name around with me is something I hadn't considered until now. It'll be a constant reminder of the strings I'm still attached to. I could always change it to my maiden name, but either way it goes, I'd be attached to some of the worst types of people on the planet — a deadbeat mother or an abusive husband.

As I walk into the jetway, I tell myself *it's only a name*. The gate shuts on me like a cell in prison, but to me, it feels like my first bit of freedom.

I'm still catching my breath as I do the walk of shame down the aisle to my seat. The eyes of fellow passengers land on me, lighting me on fire with paranoia as if they know exactly who I am, what I'm running from, or the mission I'm trying to accomplish. The unknown I'm taking off into.

I toss my bag into an overhead bin in slow motion, stalling away from the moment ahead where I have to ask two very comfortable people to let me into my window seat. When I do, I immediately lean against the panel of the plane and curl into myself like a snail on dry land. My face hides inside the hood of my sweatshirt. I turn as far to the window as anatomically possible.

In favor of being covert, the flight crew turns the lights down low, a benefit to a red-eye flight I didn't think about — difficult to see, and all anyone wants to do is sleep.

As we ascend, the last decade of my life glistens in the city lights beneath. It contaminates my mind with a recollection of events I wish I could erase.

I think about what life was like before Denver held any part of my memory. It's even more dooming to realize that once I make it to Chicago, I will feel the same about there, too.

The plane continues into the night sky, separating farther and farther from the city lights until we are flying entirely over the terrain. The terrain Ezra always warned me of. He said if I were to go missing, the vastness of the land and the treacherousness of the mountains would make it nearly impossible for me to be found. That was if anyone noticed my disappearance in the first place. I hope he's right about that.

I slide the window shutter down and flutter my eyes closed as the turbulence bumps me into a deep sleep.

Chapter 13

"Vivian?" An inquisitive voice pierces my ears from behind. I attempted to scurry away from baggage claim where I picked Nina up, but I guess it wasn't fast enough. A hand catches onto my shoulder.

"No way is that you." I barely recollect her face before the arms of Julie Pips swaddle me. "I *knew* I heard your name on the overhead speakers. I'm so glad I could catch you before leaving. What are you doing in Chicago, of all places?"

I release my bag from one hand. It falls to the floor as my other holds Nina's carrier. My heart hardens, and my chest feels like it just caved into itself. I can't form words. *Breath, Vivian. Breath.*

"Julie!" Julie Pips, the wife of John Pips – one of Ezra's golfing buddies. I finally respond with forced enthusiasm splintering my voice. "*What am I doing here?* What are *you* doing here?" I tap her shoulder playfully, dancing around her question.

"I'm here for a work conference for the next few days. What brings you all the way to Chicago, and why did it require a cat to accompany you?" She laughs, teasing me sarcastically. She's adamant about an answer as she eyes Nina.

The last thing I prepared myself for was an excuse for why I left. I only had a reason. A reason Ezra was adept at hiding from outsiders. Julie would never guess the conditions of our marriage.

Think. Think. Think. My brain churns for what is too long for Julie to stand. Her chin drops, and her forehead wrinkles ripple with curiosity. Under pressure, I finally think of a fabrication to pitch, but I hope it's enough to decoy her. My eyes drop to my feet, and my teeth nibble on my bottom lip. I slip into a melodrama, deceiving her.

"It's my mom." I blink back counterfeited tears. "Her health took a turn for the worst recently. I came to Chicago to soak up as much time as possible with her – however much of it we have left." Julie gasps and crosses her arms. She shakes her head with sadness.

"As far as her," I lift Nina's carrier slightly, "I know better than to leave a pet with Ezra for long. He can barely take care of himself, let alone a cat." I let out a soft laugh to lighten the moment. I sniffle back the lie and wipe my tears.

Although this is untruthful, I don't feel bad about lying about my mother's health. For all I know, she really could be sick. Or maybe even dead.

"Vivian, I'm so sorry to hear about your mother. I lost mine last year, and it's no cliche saying that it's one of the most difficult things you'll ever go through." OK. Maybe I do feel slightly bad about my lie now. "But you know what," she says as if she has a solution, "let's exchange numbers. You can call me any time." Julie takes her phone from her purse and hands it to me to input mine.

My heart is doing that thing again where it's bracing for my chest to cave.

Even though I don't know the number to the phone Sasha gave me, there's no way I'd give it to Julie anyway. I input a random ten-digit combination. "Thank you, Julie. I appreciate that. We'll stay in touch." I hand her the phone, and we say our goodbyes, knowing she will never hear from me again.

Because it's the middle of the night, it will be hard to get an early check-in at a hotel. After I find an ATM to deposit my cash into, I find a secluded place to sit. The airport is desolate.

I rest into a chair tucked away in the corner of a closed coffee shop. I research hotels and decide on a conveniently placed, low-priced room in downtown Chicago with an early check-in option of 7 a.m.

Until then, I nod in and out of sleep, trying to pay close attention to my surroundings. I don't want anyone else to recognize me.

Chapter 14

I wave down taxi drivers as if rushing to get to my sick mother.

One driver cringed at the sight of a cat, but when the next accepted my ride, I glided my body into the backseat with relief. Soon enough, I would be tucked into a hotel room away from any potential familiar faces.

"Where are you headed today, ma'am?"

I read verbatim from the Google search I made earlier. "The Pixy Hotel, please."

We exit the terminal and get onto the highway, where the taxi comes bumper to bumper with the car in front of us. Everyone wishes they would've left earlier before the morning rush hour. Impatient drivers honk at one another, weaving from lane to lane like a set of yarn hooks as if the blinker signal was never invented.

Working our way closer to downtown, the buildings grow wider and taller, towering over. It gives me the sensation of a tight hug welcoming me home.

I don't know whether it's the thought of being here in Chicago, that someone has already recognized me, or if it's morning sickness, but nausea works its way up to the pit of my stomach. I know I only have a few seconds before I hurl into the backseat of the taxi. I manage to yell to stop the car in time before swinging the door open to relieve myself, almost smacking the car in traffic next to us.

The driver probably wishes he would have declined my ride as the other taxi driver did. The rest of the ride is gawky and silent.

I do him a favor and ask to be let out a few blocks short of the hotel at a convenience store. I load up on snacks for me and essentials for Nina, only buying items on sale or clearance.

My walk to the hotel with a duffel bag, a cat, and shopping bags is hectic. I'm out of breath. My body feels crooked as I go through the lobby, doing my best to shield Nina from being noticed. The front desk agent checks me into my hotel in haste, probably feeling too bad for me to realize I have just smuggled a cat into a pet-free hotel.

Sweeping that worry under a rug, I make my hotel room feel like home. I turn on the TV for background noise. I fill the dresser drawers with my clothes, rest a pillow on the floor in a corner for Nina to cuddle on, and stuff snacks and water into the fridge. Feeling slightly disgusted, I pour litter into a box from the convenience store. I'll have to be sure to keep a do-not-disturb sign hung on the outside of the door. Otherwise, my plan could go to shit. Quite literally.

Running out of things to keep me busy, I call Sasha. The only number programmed in my contact list, as she said. The line rings a couple of times and then a few more before reaching her voicemail.

I'm surprised by her not answering but relieved because all I want to do is sleep away the running list of priorities I have bumping against each other – get a job, find a home, and have a baby.

Chapter 15

My eyes creak open like an aged door to an abandoned house at the sound of an unfamiliar noise. The golden-hour sun leaks through the curtains and shines directly into my eyes. The noise continues, and I finally realize it's my phone ringing for the first time.

I frantically push myself up by my fists on the bed and accept Sasha's call. "Hey! I was wondering how long we were going to play phone tag."

"I'm so sorry I missed you. I was working a double at the bar. How was the flight in?"

I sigh, relaxing my body back onto the bed. "It's been a mess. I almost didn't make it in time. Nina ended up squished somewhere under the plane, and my full name was called overhead numerous times in warning. A passenger recognized my name. She's a mutual friend of Ezra and mine."

"That's the last thing you needed. Please tell me she doesn't know what you're doing in Chicago." Concern filters through her voice.

"Of course not. I told her I was in town taking care of my dying mother."

"Well played," she praises me.

"Not really. Soon, she will know I lied to her because word

will circulate the grapevine as it always does." I rub a hand over my face in stress. "When she learns that I slithered out of the house without Ezra's knowledge, leaving everything behind, she will put the pieces together and could be a solid source of the truth about where I went. I haven't even been gone for a full day, and I already feel caught." I ramble, digging myself into a hole of regret and doubt. "Maybe you were right. Coming to Chicago was the last thing I should've done. Escaping to the city of my roots, the first place he would guess I went, seems like the dumbest choice I could have made. I feel like I made this too easy for him."

Sasha cuts me off with a lecture. "Stop it. Don't talk like that. This is not about you anymore. You made the only right decision that you knew how. Not only yourself but your child. Your number one responsibility right now is growing a healthy baby. Being paranoid and panicked will only make it harder on your pregnancy."

My hand meets my stomach, caressing my bump that barely protrudes. "It's hard staying positive. I'm scared. Scared of Ezra for what he's capable of, scared of myself for what I'm *not* capable of, and scared of a baby that's going to trust with every fiber of their being that I am capable of what they need." Nina jumps onto the bed and curls into my lap as if she senses my fear.

"If you say capable one more time, I'm going to scream," Sasha says, and we laugh. It alleviates the seriousness of our conversation for a moment.

"Vivian, the fact that you're scared of your ability to be a good mother already makes you an exceptional one. Do you think bad parents are scared of being bad parents?"

Sasha's comment infests my thoughts of my mother. I don't

know if there was a single day she tried her best to be a good parent. Did she care enough to feel as scared as I do of parenthood? Probably not. Sasha makes a good point.

"Do yourself a favor and stop being paranoid of Ezra. Chicago is a big enough city to swallow you up, absorbing you into society. Do you know how much work it would take for him to find you? Besides, now he has more free time to focus on the mistress you were telling me about."

My stomach ties into knots as I think about his late nights, the silver car dropping him off, and my skeptical conversation with Claire Bluff. Why do I even care?

"I don't want to talk about this anymore."

"I'm sorry for being harsh. I shouldn't have said that." Sasha apologizes. "Worry about the important things, like setting up a doctor's appointment. Have you done that yet?"

"No. I've slept away the business hours of any available clinic near me. Don't worry, though. I'll do it in the next couple of days." My phone dings against my ear with an incoming text. It's from Sasha. "What's this?"

"A link to a list of walk-in clinics," she says. "I'm sure a bus or train can easily get you to one of these from where you are."

"Sasha," I say her name appreciatively as I scroll through my options. "Thank you for being so helpful."

"Anything for you," she says, and I believe her. "Get some rest. I'll check on you tomorrow."

"Wait!" I catch her before hanging up.

"What's up?"

"Why?" I ask plainly.

"What do you mean *why?* Why what?"

The enigmatic facets of Sasha swarm in my mind. Understanding her is like going to an arcade and playing on the claw machine. Right when you think you got something out of her, it slips from the cranes, falling back down into everything else she doesn't want you to know.

"Why do you feel so inclined to help me? To know from the get-go that I would have needed you years later is. . ." I try to articulate my words in a way that won't pry too hard like Julie Pips did to me in the airport. "I guess what I'm trying to say is, what makes you want to be so supportive? It's a burden."

She lets out an audible exhale. "You know this. You were always my favorite employee. I gravitated to you. I hated to see you go, especially at the hip of a man like Ezra." Her answer is straightforward enough to believe, making me feel stupid for asking. "Like I said before, just take the blessing," Sasha demands. "I'll talk to you later."

We end the call, and I am left fantasizing about Ezra's paces through the house, wondering how I did it. Throwing one of his adult tantrums and punching the walls with additional holes — each of them serving as one of many reasons we could never have visitors to our home. That was probably by design.

Taking my phone meant taking his ability to track me — something he became addicted to. He's surely regretting that now.

If only I could be a fly on the wall to see his reaction, but I don't have to be anywhere near to know that he will find the audacity somewhere inside of his insidious body to pull a victim card. He will make everyone wonder why I would ever leave Denver's renowned plastic surgeon behind at the height of his career.

His charm, the same phenomenon that reeled me in and entangled me in the depths of his deceit, will be the reason why everyone will believe whatever lies he tells. When someone is anything like Ezra, alluring, confident, and successful, yet equally devious and calculated, they can harmonize with just about anyone. They morph themselves into whoever their audience wants to believe them to be, swindling them like a con artist.

The falsity he will spread makes me wish he would have disappeared instead of me. Or better yet, die and go away forever, relieving me and the rest of the world of his malevolence.

I wonder for a moment if I could have pulled it off, and if I didn't, could I have handled the rest of my life facing the consequences in prison? I think *probably*, given the circumstances of my life thus far.

Taking the anger of my lifetime out on him, creating a questionable scene the detectives of Denver had ever examined. Me as their prime suspect and proudly admitting they were right.

I close my eyes tightly and shake my head, convincing myself I would never be capable of that. Besides, as evil as Ezra is, I would be surprised if I were the only one on earth who hates him the way I do.

Maybe Claire Bluff, or whoever his mistress is, will learn to harden her heart and arm herself against him the way I have. She can end him instead.

Chapter 16

At the closest walk-in clinic on the list that Sasha sent me, a line of people had already formed by only eight in the morning.

A one-legged man rolls himself in a wheelchair. The mother in front of him cuddles her sick toddler in a onesie pajama set, sniffling between his whooping coughs. But the woman standing directly in front of me is what mostly captures my attention.

The ends of her brunette hair stretch down to the top of her mid-sized pregnant belly. Like me, she's alone, and her ring finger is naked. I can't help but wonder if her situation is anything like mine.

She whips her head over her shoulder as if she can feel me staring at her from behind. Our eyes snag onto one another and hold for a few beats. It's almost as if hers mirror mine – glossed with pain and paranoia.

When you have endured a certain level of misery and heartache like I have, you can sense and identify it anywhere.

"I can help the next person here!" The receptionist calls out, and it's at that moment I notice a Marilyn Monroe type of mole on the right side of her face before we finally peel our eyes apart. She's still stunningly beautiful through an expression that screams *get me out of here.*

For the rest of our time in line, her head darts to and from each wall of the room as if she's hyper-aware of her surroundings. Once she's checked in, my gaze follows her to where she takes a seat in the farthest corner of the waiting room she could find.

"Ma'am," a drowned voice in my mind says. Then again. "Ma'am!" The receptionist's voice interrupts my observation. My neck nearly cracks as I turn to face her and stride to the check-in desk.

"Sorry!" but I don't think she accepts my apology. She makes narrow eye contact, smacks her gum with sass, and speaks to me in a rush.

"Your name, please."

"Vivian Bozzelli." Saying his last name feels like the devil himself escaping from my mouth like shards of glass. It almost physically pains me.

She asks me for additional details and directs me to the waiting room. "A nurse will call for you within the hour."

"I'm sorry. Did you say an hour?" I question impatiently.

"Yes. This is a walk-in clinic, so the schedule fills up quickly. You can come back tomorrow when we open, and you could have little-to-no wait, although I can't promise that either."

I know I will keep putting this off if I don't do it today, so I decline and find a seat in the waiting area positioned in the direction of the woman who stood in front of me in line.

Pulling a book from my bag and opening it to a random page, I use it as a prop. I peek up from it periodically to monitor her body language — stiff, vigilant, and distrustful of her surroundings.

Chapter 17

Fifteen weeks, twenty-five weeks left until my due date. The mysterious woman in the lobby is only a fragment of my imagination. Tears crowd my eyes until there's no space left for them. I spin through the revolving door out of the clinic that spits me into the windy city. I almost ram into a pedestrian. "Excuse me," but the man dressed in a gray suit, carrying a leather briefcase, ignores me in a hurry, unphased by me.

I don't know why I'm reacting this way – surprised or disoriented. I knew I was pregnant. The test I took told me so. The small bump is undeniable validation. But there is something about the words of a professional telling me so that makes it feel too real to grasp.

Hotel living, a nonexistent support system, and joblessness; all conditions unfit for motherhood send me into a downward spiral.

A part of me feels like a failing mother already. I went months wondering if I was pregnant but ran away from the truth. To go this long without a doctor's visit feels criminal, but it would have made it too easy for Ezra to catch on if I had gone any sooner.

Sasha's words ring through my ears from our conversation

last night. *Vivian, the fact that you're scared of your ability to be a good mother already makes you an exceptional one. Do you think bad parents are scared of being bad parents?*

Speak of the devil, my phone rings. I slip it out of the bag I got from the convenience store and see that it's Sasha. Not in the mood to speak, my thumb decisively clicks the red *decline* button on the screen.

I walk past a coffee shop emitting a smell of locally roasted beans and espresso, followed by a clothing boutique. I whip my body around the corner to the train station when my phone rings again, but I don't give in. *Decline,* my thumb goes, but her name appears once more – this time as a text message.

Sasha: Urgent. Please call me back as soon as you can.

Guilt blazes through me. The only reason I have a phone is because of Sasha, so not answering her feels wrong, but I know she will understand when I express how I'm feeling right now.

Plus, I'm about to miss the train.

My inner thighs chafe with each quick step as I run to the platform before squeezing my way into the train doors just before it's too late. My hand grasps onto the pole in the aisle, and my body jerks at the train's departure. Off the strength of memory, I take the Red Line, a route that will transport me directly into familiarity. A part of the city that raised me.

For the first time ever, the neighborhood I grew up in sounds like the most comforting place in the world.

The unrhythmic, anxious beats of my heart are replaced with exciting thumps. My mouth salivates at the thought of a diner in the neighborhood that possesses some of the few memories I have worth remembering.

James Pierce, my high school sweetheart who used to hold onto my money for me and away from my thieving mother, took me there for our first date. The burgers were three dollars apiece, and a basket of fries was two bucks, perfect for a couple of broke high school kids.

He took me there every Friday from then on out. On our first Friday, we ate shyly together. The second we held hands. The third we kissed. By the fourth, we were exclusive, and our notorious orders went without saying.

My head swivels back and forth, taking in the faces and bodies of fellow train riders. As much as I would hate to breathe the same air as anyone who remembers me right now, there is one face I wouldn't mind seeing.

James'.

A decade later, I still think of how it made me feel when he decided to leave for law school, stepping in line in his father's footsteps. As a teen, I couldn't wrap my head around how anything else could be more important than us – our puppy love was the only reason I knew real love existed. As an adult, I get it now. Leaving for better. Leaving for what you want. Leaving for what you know you deserve.

Instead of his face, I look around at the view of people from all walks of life. Some are dressed business casual for their corporate jobs, while other less fortunate bodies slump into their seats, nodding in and out of a high. Then there's me, somewhere in the middle.

The train approaches my stop, and I hop off. With the option to go left toward my mother's house, I stride to the right down Marshfield Avenue to the diner. The comfort I so badly needed washes over me.

Street names come back to me like an old friend. Familiar

houses still stand along this road. Perhaps coming to Chicago was the right thing to do after all.

I even remember how my stomach would gargle at the smell of French fries and cheese-layered burger patties as James and I neared closer, hands clasped – puppy love. I feel pathetic reminiscing about him, but I can't help being taken back to those days.

The pitiful feeling burns through my chest when I reach the end of Marshfield Avenue, where the diner used to stand.

Used to.

There is no smell of fries or burgers. The neon, inviting sign that used to illuminate *open* has no window to hang on the other side. The door that used to ding with welcoming charms, the red, old-school bar stools, the black and white, retro-checkered tile, the hospitable cooks and servers. Everything is gone and replaced by a field of overgrown grass and sporadic weeds.

I feel like I'm in a foreign place.

An athletic pedestrian on a run approaches me on the sidewalk, so I step onto the uneven grass for them to pass by. The breeze from their speed makes one of my curls blow to the side of my face.

I wish I could run and keep running until I'm too exhausted to feel anything. It makes sense why people become addicted to it – it's too strenuous to think about anything other than the gallops of your feet and controlling your breath.

What was like an exciting field trip quickly changed direction. It feels like a waste of money. Money that I don't have an endless supply of.

Tears succumb to me, warranted by destitution. Everything is so familiar yet completely different at the same time. I can only imagine what more has changed.

The people I remember have likely migrated to other zip codes, states, or countries. Establishments are demolished. Things are just. . .different.

The tears begin to flow incessantly, and my heart rate accelerates, causing my breaths to become rapid, shallow, and heavy. It's a combination that binds me into a panic. My mouth is dry as if I chewed on cotton balls.

The openness around me closes in on my chest, making me feel too noticeable and dangerously vulnerable to my surroundings, almost as if Ezra is watching somewhere in the distance. Laughing that I thought I could pull this off. My arms wrap around my body, and my head falls as I speed walk back to the train station.

My phone rings in my bag, but I let it go until it stops. I already know it's Sasha. I will call her when I can breathe again.

Chapter 18

Complaining and self-pity won't get me anywhere.

The bar across the street from my hotel strikes my attention with a generic hiring sign taped to the glass of the door.

Before crossing over to the other side of the street, I wait a few extra seconds for impatient drivers to make impulse decisions at the intersection. I know better than to be an unaware pedestrian in this bustling city.

The handles of the doors are artistically made of beer bottles. I tug on them, and rock music pours out of the bar and into my ears.

"Welcome to Tony's Tap!" A tiny voice yells over the tunes.

"Hi," I greet before getting straight to my point. "I see a hiring sign on the door. Is a manager available?" I ask the host. She's cute and petite.

"Sure! I will grab him. But first, I'm Lily," she chirps, holding her hand out for a friendly shake.

I extend my arm out until my hand is in hers. "Vivian – it's nice to meet you."

Her eyes smile at me, falling in line with the affable grin of her mouth. "I'll be right back." Lily walks to the kitchen at the far side of the bar.

After a few minutes, a guy follows her from the back of the house. I paste a smile on my face at the sight of him, but not one as amorous as Lily's. Her pupils grow as they dazzle at him. The two of them approach me, and the manager introduces himself.

"Hey there," he says with a lazy undertone. "I'm Tony. Meet me on a stool at the bar."

Off the first impression, if cool, calm, and collected were personified, it would be Tony.

I find a bar stool, thankful for the ability to hide my barely visible pregnant belly behind a bar top. It also feels good to take a comfortable seat after the journey I've been on today.

"What can I get you to drink?" he asks as he glides through the bar graciously, wiping a cup dry for my beverage of choice. The way he moves is appealing. I can see why Lily stares at him the way she does.

My phone vibrates in my bag, but I ignore it. "Water would be great, thank you." I look around the establishment at customers. So far, so good. Nobody recognizes me.

Tony lays a napkin down before setting my glass of water on top and slicing a straw into it. "So, tell me. Why do you want to work at Tony's Tap?" He leans his body over the other side of the bar, his muscular forearms resting there as he stares into me for a response.

To help me answer his question, I observe my surroundings to pluck something from the decor. An award dangles from above the entrance for *the best mom-and-pop bar and restaurant in Chicago.* I shift my attention from the frame and directly back to him.

"The family history. I thrive when I'm working behind a passion. It's not something you get at an establishment run by a corporate team." I break our eye contact and glance around again, portraying a look of vehemence.

He ignores my soppy answer. "What position are you interested in?"

"Bartending. I have over a decade of experience, but I'm happy to start as a server and work my way up."

"Perfect," he lifts himself with a sigh and slaps his hands on the bar top. "We're down by one since I had a bartender call it quits last week." He reaches behind him and grabs a menu. "Take this with you and come back tomorrow. You'll need to be familiar with our taps and cocktails. Come by at noon, and you'll be ready by the time our happy hour rush starts at six." He turns his back to me, pointing at the line of spouts. "We have a total of 26 taps. The first six are seasonal, the ten in the middle are locally brewed, and the last ten at the end are commercial taps."

Amazed at how easy this was, I nod enthusiastically. "Oh. Yes. For sure. Thank you!" I fumble through my words. "I will be back at noon tomorrow."

"Cool. Bring two forms of identification, and I will get you set up on payroll. It'll take a few weeks before you can get your first check, but you'll leave out of here with your cash tips every night," Tony assures me.

"Sounds good to me," I say with too much excitement. For something like this to fall right into place when everything else is falling apart, I don't care if I sound embarrassingly eager.

I gulp the rest of my water before spinning around on the bar stool to leave.

"Oh, hi!" I say to Lily as she beams at me with excitement. How long has she been standing here?

"Congratulations! You're now what we call a *Tapper,*" she

pats my shoulder. "Sit back down. I have something for you." I listen to her hesitantly and watch her closely as she walks around to the other side of the bar where Tony just was.

Her hair is slicked into a bun so far back that it looks like it hurts. After disappearing for a moment underneath the bar, Lily pops up with two shot glasses, lining them side-by-side. "We have a tradition. Whenever a new *Tapper* joins the team, someone has to take a shot with them."

My face rises in temperature, and heat burns through my skin. "Oh, no, thank you."

"Oh, come on!"

"Are you peer pressuring me?" I ask with a grin.

Lily tilts her head to one side, and her bun pokes out from behind her head. "No. I'm not peer-pressuring you. I'm just being a *peer.*"

I laugh at her pun. "Really, I'm okay. I should get going." And I really should. I owe Sasha a call back.

Lily's back humps as she hunches over with disappointment and glares at me. "Hm. I know what it is. You're pregnant, aren't you?"

I blink back a guilty expression. Is it that noticeable? I didn't think it was easy to tell already. I look down at my stomach and readjust my shirt.

"Ha! I was only teasing you, but that was a dead giveaway! I only said that because this same thing happened before." *That's rude,* I think to myself, but she's young, so I'll give her a pass.

"Don't worry. I won't say anything to a single soul." She reaches into the collection of bottles and grabs a light liquor. "Isn't it sad?" she says, twisting the cap off, "women have to hide their pregnancy so they won't get turned away for a job." Her words make me paranoid about who might be listening in. She pours both shot glasses full. "Stop looking so nervous! Your secret is safe with me, but only under one condition." Lily slides one of the shot glasses toward me. "You have to take a shot with me," her eyebrows raise in question and then fall back to normal as her head tilts back with an innocent laugh. She takes down her shot without a grimace, then stretches across the horizon of the bar, swiping the shot she slid to me, and takes that one down like a champ, too. "Congratulations, Vivian."

The amount of emotions she's made me feel in the last thirty seconds is remarkable yet annoying. "Very funny." I laugh with relief and punch my arm through the loop of my bag. "Thank you, Lily. I will see you tomorrow." I stand on my feet, readying myself for the door.

"Wait! One more thing," she stops me, "I think the guy waiting for you outside left already."

My entire body stiffens. "What *guy?*"

"Never mind me! Maybe I was seeing things," Lily says. But I don't think she was. I leave our conversation behind and jog to the other side of the street to my hotel.

Reaching for the door handle as fast as I can feels relieving. I let out a sigh when the fresh air of the hotel lobby hits my face. My back hurts, I'm out of breath, and I need to use the bathroom more than ever. I guess this is what happens when there is a fetus resting beside your bladder.

I forget my urge to go when a voice calls out my name.

It's deeper than I remember, yet somehow still recognizable. My eyes grow wide, and the hair on the back of my neck stands up. My strides grow bigger, and my pace becomes brisk.

"Vivian!" His footsteps creep up behind me, and before I know it, his face appears over my shoulder. "I knew that was you."

I do the best I can to hide my baby bump.

Chapter 19

I guess the city of Chicago wasn't big enough to absorb me into society and make me unnoticeable after all.

My entire body flushes its blood and goes stiff at the man now standing in front of me.

He has an unrecognizable beard, but behind that is the smooth skin I remember all too well. His body is filled out with muscle rather than the bones I last remember. His voice penetrates me just as it did a decade ago.

James Pierce.

I don't say anything. Our arms wrap around each other. I lose myself in his hold. "What are you doing back?" James asks.

I'm not sure how much more I can handle in one day. I tell the same lie I told Julie Pips at the airport. "My mom. She hasn't been doing well." The lie slips from my lips with ease this time.

James tilts his head and frowns. "Is she sick?"

"Something like that." I avoid a solid answer, not wanting to lie to him any more than I already have.

"Well then, what are you doing at a hotel? Wouldn't you want to stay with her?"

"This is the least I can do. It's also the *most* I'm willing to do." I subtly remind him of what kind of mother she was before changing the trajectory of this conversation. "What are you doing here?"

"I work right around this area. But you're right about your mom. It's just. . ." he shakes his head as if he wants to say something but decides to bite his words back instead. "You know what? It doesn't matter. I'm just happy to see you. I'm sorry it's under these circumstances."

He drops his hands into the pockets of his dark blue jeans and looks down at his feet while licking his lips. A lot has changed. His mannerisms are *not* one. I know what's next. "How long are you in town for?"

"I booked a one-way ticket, but hopefully not too long. I have to get back home eventually." My insides cringe at that tale. Although I needed to tell it, the toxic part of me wanted to see how he was affected by the idea that I have lived a whole other life since he decided to leave. I want to see if it pierces through him.

His eye twitches. It worked. To protect his feelings, he avoids further questions. "Burgers from the diner this Friday?" he invites me, and my mouth salivates as it did at the thought of it earlier today, but I break the news to him about it being gone.

"I don't know how long you've been back, but I went today. Not only did they close it down, it was demolished. The lot is blooming with weeds."

James' head nods down with a laugh of mastery. He raises his eyebrows back up at me. "I've been back long enough to know they closed down the original location and moved downtown. It's not too far from here, actually," he says matter-of-factually with his well-manicured index finger pointing toward the door. He turns to face me again and delves into his back pocket for something. "We have a lot of catching up to do. Here, put your number in my phone." He passes his cell to me, forcing it into my hands.

I stare down at the screen of it and back up at James. Again, I have no idea what my number is. I hand it back to him and find my way out of it.

"James, this is too much for me right now. I need to focus on my mom and work on getting back home." *Home.* I laugh to myself in my head as I tell that lie in the lobby of what *is* my home for the time being.

His eyes deflate, and he steps closer to me. "Listen, I know that hurt you when I left, but Vivian, looking back, we were basically kids. Let this be our chance to end on a better note."

Avoiding a gushy conversation that is wrong to have as I carry the child of another man unknowingly to either one of them, I dodge his proposal. "Are you a lawyer like you always wanted?"

He sighs, looking up at the ceiling. "Divorce attorney."

For some reason, his response makes me wince. "Well, good. It was worth it. I'm happy for you."

"Please, Vivian," he begs, but as if I am saved by a bell, my phone rings for what feels like the millionth time today.

I reach past the appointment summary document and ultrasound photos I have yet to look at from my visit to the clinic and grab my phone from my bag. As expected, it's Sasha.

"I'm sorry, James. I need to take this. It was great seeing you. Just don't creep up on me like that again. Or follow me around and watch me from a distance in a bar."

His lips tuck into each other, and he blinks a few times. "What are you talking about? I wasn't watching you." He seems confused as all can be, but I don't press him about it.

"I got to go, James. I'm sure I'll see you again." I turn around on my heels. I can feel James' eyes burn into me as I walk to the elevator, accepting Sasha's call.

"Hello?" I answer as I press the *up* button while glancing over my shoulder and back at James. I give him a final slight smile and wave.

"Why the hell haven't you been answering my calls or texts?!" Sasha yells into the phone, snatching me out of the moment with James and into her world of consternation.

I've never heard Sasha sound this frantic before. "Relax! I went to the doctor this morning and found a job, and you would never believe who I just ran into. I'm just now making it back to my hotel," I say as the elevator dings upon arrival. I step inside. "It's been a long day," I attempt to explain.

Sasha continues with her rant. "You have no idea. . ." the phone cuts out as the elevator lifts to the fifth floor. "Claire Bluff. . ." I can barely make out Sasha's words through the rough service connection, but that name alone catches my attention.

"Sasha, I just got into the elevator. I will call you right back."

Her voice shakes as she continues anyway. "News channel. . ." the line crackles. "Found dead. . .being questioned." The call dies out and fails, but I hang onto her last words.

Claire Bluff.

Found dead.

Chapter 20

The minute I exit from the elevator, I call Sasha back.

The phone barely rings once before she answers and picks up where she left off. "What type of situation did you get me into, Vivian?"

I beg her to slow down and rewind to the beginning. "Please just relax and tell me what is going on." I insert my room key into the slot on the door and slam it shut behind me. "Did you say Claire Bluff is *dead?!*"

My mind is taken aback by what I'm hearing but also by the smell of cat feces and urine. *Oh my god,* I say under my breath. Nina whines as she approaches me at my feet, clearly feeling neglected.

"No, Vivian! Listen to me right now. Ezra. . .was. . .found. . .DEAD. Claire Bluff is on national television sobbing, asking the public for answers. Tell me right now what the hell is going on!" But I can't.

My knees go weak, and my entire body numbs into nothing. My palm reaches to my chest, and my other hand hardly braces my fall. The phone bounces to the ground in what looks like slow motion. I can hear Sasha's loud words through the speaker of the phone, but her voice is distant and faint from afar.

The pain of losing someone I thought I would have celebrated the death of, combined with all the pain that same person caused, wails out of me. I lose my breath between cries. When? How? Maybe this would have never happened if I never left.

Vivian! Hello? Hello-o? Sasha's voice still sounds far out in the distance. A knock on the door echoes from what I can only guess is a concerned guest, and Nina meows in concern.

Once I manage to compose myself, I locate my phone where it fell to the floor. Nina curls into my lap as I rest on the ground. I still can't stand.

I bring the phone to my ear and let out a shaky breath, still hysterical. It's hard to speak without cracks in my voice. "What do they think happened to him?"

"They aren't providing details to the public, but they expect foul play, so you tell me! He didn't show up for surgery the morning after you left. I was brought in for questioning today and had zero information to provide. Authorities somehow know I dropped you off at the airport, which means they probably know you're in Chicago."

My jaw is in hell where Ezra probably is. My body freezes in time. Even the tears in my eyes freeze in motion before falling down my cheeks. I can't talk, move, or think clearly enough to make sense of this.

Sasha continues. "I don't know what you got yourself into, but I sure hope you didn't drag me into a murder investigation. You better count your dollars and lay low because the next thing you know, you'll be one of America's most wanted if this doesn't work itself out."

"Stop!" I yell. "Please, just shut up! Don't you think I understand how terrible this looks? And for you to believe I would get you involved in something so criminal, let alone be responsible for someone's death, is insulting!" I cry. "You know I would never do that, Sasha. You know me."

"I thought I did," she corrects me.

"You still do!" but the line beeps, rendering our conversation. I have never heard such disappointment in her voice. For her to not bother to ask how my appointment went or congratulate me on the job I landed is gutting.

How could she think I did something like this? I know I've had my fantasies, but I would've never set out to execute any of them.

If Sasha isn't in my corner, who will be? I have no one, and if I don't, who will my child have? Any chance of having a father has been ripped away. The likelihood of having a mother currently feels like a fifty-fifty chance if I'm going to be suspected of doing something heinous to Ezra.

The question is, who did, and why?

Chapter 21

If I'm doing the math correctly, I have about two months of finances left, but that's generous. I need to rack up as much money as fast as I can.

Instead of getting the sleep I need for my first day on the job tomorrow, it's now three in the morning, and I'm running through every possibility of Ezra's unexpected death. I found a notepad and pen in the nightstand drawer and began jotting down every scenario that came to mind.

I start by writing my name at the top of the page but cross a line through it because I obviously didn't do this. I continue with a list of possibilities.

An unknown health condition mistaken for foul play.

Claire Bluff decided she had enough of being the mistress. If she couldn't have Ezra, no one could. She even got on the news, like most killers do, to take the heat off herself.

A patient wanted revenge for a surgery gone wrong.

A burglar found his way through a window and took what he wanted, including Ezra's life.

Or maybe nobody did it. Maybe he took himself out after realizing I was gone. I left my ring on the counter, and he got the message and couldn't handle it.

The list goes on and on, but it becomes more and more

unrealistic and far-fetched the longer it grows. I list every name from myself to Sasha, down to Julie Pips – nothing is making sense.

As much as I am trying to prepare myself for an interrogation I will more than likely have to sit through, I cannot think of why anyone other than myself would have had the motive to kill Ezra. Unless, of course, it's someone I knew nothing about.

I write down the words *silver sedan* and draw a circle around it. Who dropped him off the night he came home belligerently drunk?

I am going to find out who did this. Not because Ezra deserves justice, but for my child. They need me. I'm all they will have.

Chapter 22

"Alright, tell me what's in the *Peach Fuzz*." Tony tests my knowledge of the cocktail menu that didn't get any of my attention last night as I mapped out Ezra's murder. I can barely fixate on the menu items today because of the puffiness around my eyes.

Sasha advised me to lay low, but I can't do that when my money is slowly dwindling into extinction after only a couple of days.

"Meddled peach, one shot of rum, lemonade concentrate, simple syrup, shake, coat the rim in sugar, and pour over a scoop of ice."

"Bingo," he praises me. "Last question. What is our hoppiest local beer available?"

"*Tappers IPA*," I answered with certainty.

Tony hands over a punch card and an apron to tie around my waist. He walks me through inputting orders on the computer, but my mind is too preoccupied with my dead husband to digest anything he's saying.

Before I know it, his demo is over, and I just missed everything.

"Lily!" he yells over my shoulder to her.

She turns around with a buzz of excitement. "Coming!"

"I'm heading out for a few hours until the happy hour rush. If Vivian needs any help, you know what to do."

"I know *exactly* what to do." Lily winks.

The tension grows thick. I feel like I'm standing in the middle of what's supposed to be a hidden fling. "Wait, you're leaving us here alone?" I ask Tony.

He clears his throat, standing up straighter. "I have some things I need to handle. Our server tonight, Lonnie, will be here any minute to cover the dining room. You're on duty for the bar, and Lily will be hosting, food-running, and bussing."

Lily looks at me and nods with a smile of motivation as if this is what she's used to. "Sounds good to me," I respond, but truthfully, it doesn't. I'm already starting to understand why that bartender walked out and quit last week. I've only been here for an hour, and I'm already thrown to the wolves.

After Tony leaves, Lily meets me at the bar to keep me company.

"You know my secret, so tell me yours," I insist, but she doesn't seem inclined. "It's only fair." I lean my lower back against a countertop and cross my arms over my stomach.

"I think I know what you're wondering, but I can't talk about it," Lily refuses.

"What if I give you a shot?"

It doesn't take much to please her, I guess. "Fine."

I push myself from the counter and reach under for the same bottle of white liquor she chose yesterday. I cascade it into a shot glass and position it in front of her.

Lily takes it down like a champ once again. My face curls up *for her* before she finally speaks to what she supposedly couldn't thirty seconds ago. "We're a thing."

"You and Tony?" I ask as if I didn't already know.

"Yes, but we try to hide it while at work. If people knew I was dating the owner, do you think that would go over very well?"

"Wait, so Tony is the owner?"

"Why do you think the bar is called Tony's Tap?" Lily asks me condescendingly. "He's a control freak. He would never run this place without his eyes on his employees and his hands in the mix."

"I didn't put two and two together. *Pregnancy brain*." My doctor said a foggy mind is common among pregnant women.

"That's probably why you still haven't noticed the man that was here yesterday and now again today. I thought I may have been going crazy, but when I saw him again and the same way he was watching you through the windows, I couldn't unsee it."

"Oh, I know who that was," my emotions blossomed. "My high school sweetheart discovered I'm back in town."

Lily's face looks disgusted. "I don't think your high school sweetheart would look twenty years older than you."

My heart sinks, but I have to find a way to pick it back up when a group of guys walk through the door. "We're not done talking about this," I utter sharply.

Chapter 23

When Tony said there was a happy hour rush, he meant it.

Lily had zero time to accompany me between customers as she rushed through the restaurant, seating newcomers, bussing tables, and running food. That said, I was distracted by a surprise pregnancy and a criminal case I have on my hands.

There were a few customers who seemed to search my eyes with skepticism, but I double-poured their rounds to fog whoever's face they thought they recognized.

I end the night by counting my tips, bringing me up to a total of one hundred and seventy dollars in cash for the night. Not too shabby.

The electricity that passes through me lights me on fire with a purpose I feel like I haven't had in years. The cash back transactions with Ezra's credit card at gas stations and grocery stores gave me a thieving feeling. I craved this kind of independence of making my own money again.

"You can tap out for the night," Tony insists. This must be another one of Tony's Tap slang words.

Lonnie is gone by this point, so the only people left are Tony, Lily, and I. "Is there anything I can help with to close the house down?"

"Nope, you're all good. Lily and I got it covered."

"Are you sure? I'm happy to help. Nothing has been cleaned. There is a lot to do for two people."

"I said we got it," Tony sternly reminds me.

My pregnancy brain already caused me to forget the dynamic between him and Lily, but apparently, Lonnie understands the assignment. At the end of the night, everyone leaves. I suppose I should catch onto the memo.

I try to linger around for as long as I can to get alone with Lily one last time before I leave, but I conclude that I won't be able to ask her about it tonight.

After gathering my belongings, I stay alert until I make it across the street to the hotel. With no one in sight, I think maybe Lily is overthinking whoever she saw.

Chapter 24

When I enter my hotel room, it's once again reeking of cat waste. This living space is not equipped for pets of any kind, but I have no choice but to make do. I refill Nina's bowls with water and food and clean her litter box.

Nina tails me as I locate the pieces of paper I scribbled my predictions onto last night, picking apart what could have happened to Ezra. She rubs against my body, her fur flaking onto me each time. Nina freezes. Her muzzle whips over, and her ears twitch at my phone ringing.

I scramble to my feet. It's Sasha. She wouldn't answer any of the times I called her after she hung up on me the other night.

Before answering, I consider what could be on the other end of this call. Does she want to remind me how disappointed she is in me? Give me an update on the investigation, or tell me he's not actually dead? I accept the call either way because I have my own reasons to speak with her.

"Hi," she says, sounding more forgiving than yesterday. "Can we talk?"

Relieved of her composure, my reply hankers. "Of course we can."

Sasha's voice flares, "I need to apologize for how I treated you. I should have listened to how your appointment went, congratulated you on finding a job so fast, and gave my condolences. I'm still not exactly sure what's going on, and I don't know the truth, but I do know you didn't deserve that."

My lip quivers at her apology. Having spent most of the day distracted from the sensibility of my reality, it begins to set in all over again. I selfishly forgive her quicker than she probably deserves because I need to pick her brain.

"I appreciate the apology. Emotions are running high. I'm sorry you feel like I put you into the middle of a mess, but I swear to you, Sasha. I do not know what happened."

She lets out a long sigh filled with what sounds like slight disbelief. "Vivian, there's no other way to say this. You're their number one suspect, and you made me second on their list by getting me involved with your escape."

"I'm sorry." That's the only thing that comes to mind.

"Don't be. I'm out of the weeds now. I had a sealed-tight alibi. After dropping you off, I went to the bar and worked on inventory for a few hours." After making an unforgivable inventory mistake in the past, Sasha always goes in the middle of the night when no one is working, so there are no distractions. "I'm surprised they haven't located you and brought you in for questioning yet."

My heart pulsates. "Sasha."

"What?"

I pull Nina closer to me for comfort. "I think they know where I am. Exactly where I am."

The pitch of her voice rises, and the same disappointed tone she had before makes its way back. "What have you been doing? I told you to lay low!"

"I had to go to work! I have to make money! What the hell

else am I supposed to do?" I ask her rhetorically. "But here's the thing. . .For two days in a row now, the host at the bar said that she sees a man watching me from outside the window. I thought it was James, my high school sweetheart I tried telling you about, but it's not. If Ezra wasn't dead, I would think it was him. I guess he's much older."

Sasha responds with frustration. "Don't you know what's going on?"

"Obviously not!" We sound like sisters who have spent too much time together.

"I can imagine that a death like this where a murder is suspected is federal, meaning they will go to every length to locate you, and they have extensive resources to do so. That is more than likely a detective watching your every move." Sasha's voice is stressed and begins to rasp. "Do not leave your hotel room," she barks. "Don't."

Chapter 25

Too stubborn to listen to Sasha, I came in for my second night on the job.

I don't know why she thinks I can coop up in a hotel room that isn't free. Working is not an option. Taking her advice would make me go broke, so shunning myself to a room feels irresponsible. Wouldn't that make me look guilty?

Ice cubes clank into a highball glass, and the mixture of the Peach Fuzz cocktail splashes over it. It becomes clear why this is the only drink Tony bothered to teach me. It's all anyone ever orders besides beer, which is the easy part.

The hardest part of the job isn't memorizing the drinks or food menu. It's not getting along with other staff because there aren't enough employees anyway. It's trying to stay as inconspicuous as possible, knowing my face could flash on the news at any time and make me out as a woman running from a murder I'm innocent of.

It's Friday night, so I expect tonight's rush to be even more intense than yesterday's. Before it picks up, I find Lily at the host stand.

"Hey, can I ask you a question?"

She turns around and faces me with a smirk. "Sure."

"Can you tell me more about the guy you saw?"

Lily groans like she doesn't want to talk about it anymore. "What are you so worried about? I mean, look at you, Vivian. You have a pregnancy glow out of this world. Your hair spirals with perfection. Your cheekbones are model-like. I stop and stare, too. You just don't notice it." I blush at her compliments. "You're admirable. The man was probably a creep checking you out. But I didn't see him again today. It was someone different." She raises her eyebrows with a gleam. "Now I bet *this* one was the guy you were telling me about."

She doesn't understand. Although I'm slightly relieved, I feel paranoid. If James sees me working here, the lie about me visiting to see my mom is spoiled. I don't have any lies left to give.

"How do you even notice these things?" I ask Lily.

"How haven't you? You should pay better attention to your surroundings." She points a finger over my shoulder. "Like the fact that there is a customer behind you waiting to be seated."

Embarrassed, I turn around and excuse myself, giving her space to do her job.

My guard is raised as I return behind the bar and busy myself. My hands are occupied serving drinks, my eyes absorb the faces of every guest, and my mind wanders to the thought of detectives, a courtroom, examinations, and prison cells.

And, of course, motherhood.

"Excuse me," a husky voice delivers from a stool at the end of the bar. The man points up a finger as if he's ready to order. Even with my guard up, I failed to notice him there.

I wipe the excess water on my hands onto the sides of my pants and walk over to him. "I'm sorry. I didn't see you there! What can I get for you?"

"An explanation as to what happened on the night of June

25th."

The date rings a bell instantly, and my body stiffens. Nothing moves. Everything stops.

"Detective Douglas Ranger in the homicide unit of the Chicago Police Department." He reaches his arm across to show a badge. "I am the lead detective for the death of Ezra Bozzelli. Your husband," he says with snarky confidence as he slips his badge away. "So tell me. What happened that night?"

A receding hairline, a shiny bald spot, and a beer belly; this has to be who Lily saw the first time.

I look over at the host stand. My eyes meet hers as they widen with confusion, and she shrugs her shoulders.

Shit. Shit. Shit. I should have listened to Sasha, but it's too late now. I have to face it.

Say something, Vivian. Say something.

Unoiled gears turn in my mind, creaking as I search for something believable to say. Still frozen in place.

"You have been following me around for days! This is harassment!" I hiss.

His round stomach pulses, and the creases of his eyes wrinkle with a laugh. To be able to laugh in a situation like this is evil and maybe even slightly unprofessional, in my opinion.

"Harassment? You are being suspected of murder. A federal offense. This is called investigating." Thankfully, the rock music rattles through the bar and hushes our voices.

I snap back. "Well, if that's the case, we can have this conversation in a private place. I'll tell you everything I know, although, beware, it isn't much. I didn't do what you think I did, and I don't know who did or why. But please, I need this job. If you thought I was going to give you a spiel in the middle of my workplace, you have lost your mind."

He leans over the bar with narrowed eyes. "You have until midnight to make it to the station, or you'll see what harassment *really* looks like," Detective Douglas Ranger threatens.

I mirror his non-verbal language, angling my body toward him with a squint. "I'm going to guess you have been doing this job for quite some time." I glance up at the top of his bald head. "What a rookie mistake to have not read my rights when asking a question like that. Even if I did give you any information, you wouldn't have been able to use it against me in a court of law."

The corner of his mouth twitches, and I press myself up to stand.

"Is there anything I can get before you leave, sir?"

"Again, you have until midnight." Detective Douglas Ranger leaves it at that. He struggles to peel himself away from the stool before leaving out of the side emergency exit door where he must have sneaked in.

Lily meets me where he left me standing, stunned and torpid.

"What was that all about? It looked intense!" Her chirpy, lighthearted voice is never off-key. "That's the guy I was trying to tell you about! Not the hot one," she waves her hand in dismissal. "The old creepy-looking one."

"I told him to leave me the hell alone."

I engage myself in random organizing and cleaning to avoid eye contact. I try my best to look nonchalant, although my stomach twists and turns, and my armpits are damp from nervous sweat.

I look to my left at the other end of the bar, where a new customer has just seated themselves. With an excuse not to talk about it, I shoo Lily away politely.

Chapter 26

Today's shift was the worst one yet.

Although bartending is nearly as mindless as riding a bike, and I'm leaving with cash tips of one hundred and fifty dollars after a busy Friday night happy hour, I'm not sure I can stick with it for the rest of my pregnancy. I can't keep abandoning customers for frequent vomit breaks when random smells make me ill or multiple bathroom breaks when my child pushes against my bladder.

At my doctor's appointment, the physician told me the sickness usually suppresses around twelve weeks. Being that I'm weeks past that now, it pained her to admit that it's something I'll likely deal with for the remainder of my pregnancy.

"Thank you for covering me for the rest of the night, Lonnie. I appreciate it." He was assigned to the dining room, as he seems to be every night.

"You're welcome." Lonnie is a man of very few words.

I was intimidated to ask if he would mind taking over for me because he doesn't speak much. He didn't seem to mind and was quite nice about it. Tony and Lily will make him leave early for the night anyway.

I clear off dishes from the bar top and go to the kitchen

before leaving for the night. With full hands, my foot kicks to swing the door open.

It widens at the sight of Tony and Lily standing face-to-face. For a moment, I thought I was witnessing a loving kiss or something exciting. Then I notice the finger he frantically moves from out of her face. Whatever conversation was happening just came to a screeching stop. It was nothing exciting. I would know. "Is everything alright back here?"

Lily's voice cracks through her chirps this time. "Yes. Everything is fine."

"*That looked intense!*" I say, mocking her words from earlier. Lily bites her lip and weaves her arms through each other.

"Same time tomorrow, Bozzelli," Tony says. His personality is dry, but I didn't take him to be hostile like I had just seen.

My blood bubbles up. Between his aggressiveness and calling me by my last name, I snap. Not too much, though. I need this job. On top of that, I now worry that I need to keep an eye out for Lily's safety.

"I'll be here. But, Tony, I would appreciate it if you would only call me by my first name."

Lily attempts to soothe the strain between us all. "Oh, that's just what he does. He calls everyone by their last names sometimes! It comes with being a Tapper."

I walk over to the sink and clash the dishes into it. "Please count me out of it." I reach for my purse from the hook on the wall and swing it over my shoulder. I fake a smile to them and leave them to bicker.

When I check the time on my phone, I pick up the pace on my way out of the bar after realizing I have thirty minutes to get to the police station. I push my way out of the door by the beer bottle handle. I don't get very far before his face unexpectedly appears out of nowhere.

Chapter 27

"Detective? I thought we were meeting at the station?"

"I thought you may appreciate the ride." His stance is wide. His stare is steady. "I've been watching you the past several days now. By the time you figured out which line to take on the train and everything else, you would've been late. I didn't want to have to harass you tomorrow," he snarks, "so here I am."

He calls direction to the end of the block with the point of his finger, bringing my attention to his unmarked car.

"I'm parked right down the street. What do you say?"

My feet hurt, and my back aches, but stubbornness wins. "I'd rather not," I say simply and fall silent.

Following suit, Detective Douglas Ranger plays along with my strife. We stand silently for what feels like an entire minute. It gives me time to think about the possible repercussions of my bullheaded behavior. I need to be cooperative rather than challenging his superiority.

My ego finds a way to give in but with pride.

Without explanation, I walk purposefully in the opposite direction of my hotel. When he realizes I'm headed to his car, he moves quickly to catch up.

Aside from the dent on the left side of the front bumper, the car is a crisp black and precisely clean.

When he opens his door for me, the overhead light in the front seat illuminates a photo of him and a woman smiling. They look happy together.

I make conversation as we pull away from the curb. Creating a personal connection might help.

"Is that your girlfriend?"

"That would be my wife. Detective Kelly Ranger," he says with dignity. "Together for thirty-two years and counting. She's the love of my life."

"I'm sure having an occupation in the same line of work as your spouse makes for an understanding relationship. Yes?" I'm trying to make up for the attitude I gave him by building rapport before he interrogates me.

"It does indeed." He sounds unimpressed.

Unable to think of anything else to say, I pretend to stare out the window into the city from the highway. A random smell I cannot put my finger on shocks my nose. My stomach turns, prompting my mouth to salivate.

"Pull over!" I yell.

"What? So you can run away again? Hell no. We're almost there," Detective Douglas Ranger refuses.

"Please!" I beg. "I'm about to vomit!"

But he doesn't care.

We go over several more bumps in the road and bend around a couple of corners, leading me to the brink of what I can handle.

I unbuckle my seat belt and lean over to relieve myself onto the middle of the back seat floor, barely missing myself.

"What the hell!" he yells, glaring at me in disgust through the rear view mirror. "Ugh!"

I spit out the rest of what's left over in my mouth.

"I told you to pull over!" Through my sickness, I find a sly thing to say. "Maybe you'll believe me moving forward."

Chapter 28

The walls are an ugly eggshell color, the air is as stiff as a straight jacket, and it feels below freezing in the interrogation room.

Detective Douglas Ranger presses the record button.

"You have the right to remain silent. Anything you say can and will be used against you in a court of law. You have the right to an attorney. If you cannot afford an attorney, one will be provided for you. Do you understand the rights I have just read to you?"

"Yes."

I could plead the fifth, but I'm better off speaking for myself. A rusty public defender of the state loaded with dozens of cases wouldn't have the time and attention mine would need.

"With these rights in mind, do you wish to speak to me?"

"Yes," I repeat. I smile at him like a proud mother for reading my rights this time.

His eyes roll, and he lets out a fed-up sigh.

"I'm not here to play games with you. Do you understand me? You are on the line for the murder of your husband, and you have the nerve to smile at me as if you didn't just move across the country. You're living out of a hotel and working in some random bar across the street, showing zero remorse or concern."

"Remorse for what? For leaving an abusive marriage?" He jots that down on a notepad. "I didn't do anything to my husband, although I am curious to know who did and why. Whoever did could have very well killed both of us that night if I didn't leave as soon as I did. Then you guys would be working a double homicide!"

He doesn't respond to that.

"How was he murdered anyway?"

"I can't disclose that information." He glosses over my question and reverts to the first thing I said. "So you're claiming your husband was abusive?"

"I'm not claiming he was abusive; I am telling you he was."

"And was there ever a police report filed against him?"

"Of course not. Our neighbor, Ms. Joyce, called the police after witnessing an altercation a couple of years ago. When the police came, they trusted Ezra after he talked them into believing I was crazy. I never saw the point in calling them again after that."

A way out of this comes to mind.

"You know what you should do? Talk to Ms. Joyce, the lady who lives next door."

"Oh, trust me. We have."

"And what came out of that?"

"We are unable to disclose that with you," Detective Douglas Ranger shuts me down again. "But if you had to guess, what would she have been inclined to tell us?"

"Well, for starters, she saw Sasha pick me up the night I left."

"And how do you know that?" He questions.

"We saw her. Well, I didn't, but Sasha did. I told her there was nothing to worry about. Ms. Joyce was harmless. If anything, she knew why I was leaving." He writes this down also, then drops his pen.

"Speaking of that night, walk me through it. June 25th. Tell me every detail you can remember." He leans back into his chair, folding his arms over one another and resting them on his bulging stomach.

"After Ezra left for work that morning, I left soon after. I went to the bar I used to work at, where I knew Sasha was still managing. I waited in the back alley until she came outside for a smoke break."

"I was parked there for several hours, waiting until she finally did, but she was with someone, so I couldn't bring attention to myself."

"With very little time left to wait, I pulled away. I needed to make it home before Ezra. Because if he knew I had left and where I'd gone, I didn't know how he would've reacted."

"That was when Sasha ended up coming out. We talked. I told her I needed to leave, and she booked a flight for me that night. I stopped for gas before getting home in time. I thought so, at least. When I opened the garage, Ezra's car was there, but when I went inside, he wasn't. And neither was Nina."

Detective Ranger interrupts me for clarification. "Who is Nina?"

"My cat."

He nods with understanding.

"So anyways. . .I searched the entire house for her, and she was nowhere to be found. I knew Ezra had done something to her. I didn't know what until Ms. Joyce came knocking on the door with Nina in her arms."

"By that time, her fur was sopping wet from the rain. It had been pouring all day. Ms. Joyce told me she found her wandering outside but assured me Nina didn't get out by accident, alluding to the fact that Ezra had let her out."

He pauses me again. "So you think he let the cat out because you weren't back by the time he got home? Out of spite?"

I nod vigorously. "That's *exactly* what I think." I'm getting somewhere with him. He seems more receptive, so I'm becoming more relaxed as I recall what happened.

"I knew I was leaving that night, and without knowing when Ezra would be home, I packed my bag and hid Nina in the basement so he wouldn't know I found her. It was my way of making sure he felt he was still in control."

"This is where it got interesting. As I was packing, I noticed a gun under his pillow. I wrapped it in one of his T-shirts and hid it."

Detective Douglas Ranger uncrosses his arms and sits up straighter. His elbows rest on his knees, and his hands are clasped with interest. "What kind of gun was it?"

My hands raise in unison, my lips tuck into my mouth, and I shake my head. "I couldn't tell you. I don't know a damn thing about guns. And I didn't know Ezra did either. It was news to me that he even owned one."

"Where did you hide it?"

"Inside of a box in the kitchen." My answer slithers out with relaxation. It feels good to be telling the truth. "A box to a blender."

"Why did you hide it?"

"I thought he may have planned to use it."

"Use it how?"

I respond as if it's obvious. "To kill me." Detective Douglas Ranger doesn't sympathize with me. Instead, he expects me to continue with my details. So I do.

I explain everything else. From the time he got home when the random silver sedan dropped him off drunk and demented to the final moments I had in the house. I describe the details to the best of my ability.

While he showered, I scrambled to get Nina from the basement, leave my ring on the counter, and meet Sasha outside. I even admitted to seeing Julie Pips at the airport when I landed in Chicago.

His facial expression tells me he knew that already. I knew that word would travel fast.

He asks me additional questions to clarify the details still unknown to him, filling the gaps in my story. I'm beginning to feel more and more comfortable in this conversation with Detective Douglas Ranger.

"Tell me about your friendship with Sasha, and why didn't you call her rather than wait outside of her job?"His question is filled with genuine curiosity.

"I wouldn't have wanted him to track my location as he's notorious for. Well, *was*," I correct myself. "He had been tracking me since the beginning of our relationship, but he wouldn't have been able to that day even if he wanted to. He took my phone the night before."

His head perks up. "And why was that?"

"Because I was in the bathroom with the door locked. He broke through it to get to me. That's when he took it, saying the only way he'd give it back was if I told him what I was doing. I'm sure the detectives in Denver noticed the broken door."

"Did you ever tell him?"

"No."

"Why?"

I nibble on the corner of my lip, contemplating sharing.

I conclude that for them to understand the extent of why I wanted to leave, I have to tell him.

I twist my body until my stiff spine cracks from sitting here for so long. My bag hangs on the back of the chair. I reach inside, feeling around for a copy of my appointment summary and the ultrasound photos I haven't had the courage to look at since my first appointment.

I lay both of them out on the table that separates us. My answer is silent but apparent. I hope it is, at least.

He picks up the ultrasound and takes it with him as he sits back in his seat.

As he examines the sonogram images, I provide more depth to answer his question.

"I put the test in the tank on the back of the toilet. If someone were to lift it, they'd see I'm telling the truth about that, too. I put it there when he counted to five as if I were a child, warning me he would force his way in. And he did. That was when the rest of the night unfolded."

He finally looks up from the ultrasound. I'm surprised he's taken it in for this long before finally setting it down and asking his next question.

He sighs as if it's time to get back to business.

"So you said that you left your ring on the counter. Which counter?"

"Yes. The kitchen counter to the left of the sink."

"You need to tell me the truth."

I become defensive all over again after thinking I was in the clear. I've given him more than he probably expected, every detail I could think of, and he still thinks I'm lying.

"What do you mean? I am!" My eyes swell with tears. "Are you telling me the ring wasn't there when they searched throughout the home?" A tear trickles down my face. I wipe it away fiercely.

"You know, this is the first time you've cried since we've talked about the death of your husband." He smacks his hand on the table, and I wince at his unexpected outburst. "No! There was no God damn ring. Where did it go?"

Triggered by his demeanor, I swallow the lump in my throat and talk softer in an effort to calm him down.

"Detective Ranger. . ." I hold out my left hand. "I do not have the ring on, and if you guys wanted to search my hotel room or anywhere else, you wouldn't find it! Not with me," I promise him. "Maybe you could take note of the missing ring. It could have been a burglar. Was anything else missing?"

Another light bulb beams in my mind.

"His. . .his assistant," I stutter, "Claire Bluff. I suspected something going on between them. Maybe an affair. What if she's the one who did this and took the ring obsessively? Or what if her husband found out about them and wanted him gone – killing him and taking my ring as a keepsake? Isn't that what killers do? Keep items of their victims like a sick trophy?"

His face turns crimson. He slaps the table harder this time, sending his pen rolling to the ground. He stands over me and brandishes his finger in my face.

"Listen, Vivian Bozzelli." I cringe. "Don't tell me how to do *my* fucking job! I've been doing this for a very long time. I am telling you right now, I know a guilty person when I see one, and there's one sitting right here in front of me." He steps closer, pressing his finger deeper toward my face. "You tell me some bullshit about an old lady next door who probably has an unreliable memory. You throw an ultrasound in my face, believing that would make me think you're any less capable of murder. The murder of your husband, who had every right to know he was about to be a father before he left this earth!"

He slams a fist to the wall beside me, and my arms instinctively flinch to the front of my face as I sink further into my chair.

The room stands still. I picture Ezra on the inside of my eyelids. My shoulders shake through sobs.

To treat a woman this way, interrogating or not, is wrong. To make matters worse, his behavior toward a pregnant woman opening up about her abusive, now-deceased husband, whom she abruptly escaped across the country to protect the life of her child by any means necessary, is unforgivable.

"I would like to work with a female detective for the rest of this investigation."

Chapter 29

Detective Douglas Ranger found a female cop to take me home, but I still refused a ride to the hotel after my experience with him.

Instead, I took the Red Line back downtown and was reminded of the type of people that come out at night.

A ride in the back of his police car next to my vomit would have been safer than a train ride alongside skeptical people.

By the time I got to my hotel, it was three in the morning.

Today, my head feels like it's exploding from a raging headache after the long night I had. Calling into work was something I couldn't afford, and neither could this severely understaffed bar.

Lily's voice at the host stand is an annoyance as I reminisce about how the rest of last night went.

I removed a painting from the wall of my hotel room and replaced it with the string of ultrasound photos I finally dared myself to look at. Staring at the images, clashing thoughts took over my mind.

Half of me. Half of Ezra. This baby is *ours.*

At that moment, I realized I hated him as much as I loved him. And I hate that.

Wanting him out of my life and wanting him off this earth

are two different things. I felt heavy with contradictions.

It's hard to be sad when I think of everything he put me through, but moments like that are conflicting.

I spent several more hours awake, writing the possibilities of what could have happened to Ezra.

Ms. Joyce. I drew a line through that. She's too frail and sweet to ever do such a thing.

Sasha. I wrote her name in desperation of trying to pin this on someone but crossed a line through her name, too. She has a time-stamped alibi.

A family member. Ezra never told me about any of his family (another red flag I let slide), only that most of them live in Italy. It's possible one of them had a reason good enough to come to the States and do this to him. I didn't cross that possibility out, but I didn't draw a circle around it either. It felt like a stretch.

I wrote *silver sedan* and circled those words once again.

I stand behind the bar in deep thought and fatigue as I think through all these scenarios.

The door at the entrance swings open, and Lily's voice pings my ears. "Welcome to Tony's Tap! Would you like a seat at the bar or dining area?"

A deep, familiar voice responds and travels up my spine. "The bar, please."

I adjust my apron to try and better hide my baby bump, which becomes a little less forgiving to my clothes every day.

James approaches the bar and dramatically clears his throat, letting his presence be known.

I wipe the metal edges of the ice machine and every other random thing around to keep me occupied and avoid looking up at him.

"Is this how you treat all of your customers?" James breaks

our silence. "Like they're invisible."

My hands ball into fists and travel to my hips as I stare at him, feeling busted.

He looks around, making sure no one can hear him. Lily stares in our direction with a teasing smile, but we both ignore her.

"Vivian, I know you're not just here to visit. You've been staying in a hotel and now have a job. I may be a lot of things, but you know I'm not stupid." I twist my head away from him and inhale a gulp of air with a roll of my eyes. "And you're not here for your mom."

My head spins to observe his face, looking for a joking expression. He's serious, though.

"How would you know that?"

With his hands clasped together, James' eyes close. He licks his lips. I wish he wouldn't do that.

"I moved back last year. You were non-existent on social media, and everyone from back in the day lost touch with you too." His fingers separate from each other, and his hands go up as if he's at a loss for words. "I went to your mom's. Okay? Don't be mad, but I wanted to see you. I wanted to know how you've been."

My heart aches a little at the thought of my mom. A pit in my stomach forms when I think of how terrible of a daughter I am for James to have seen her, and I still haven't.

"Oh yeah? Did she ask about me?" I feel hopeful for a moment. Hopeful that she cares. But when doesn't answer me, my guilt washes away. "She didn't even react at the sound of my name, did she?"

He tries to beat around the truth. "All she said was that you packed up and went away for college. She hasn't heard from you since."

"Did she seem to care?"

He looks down at nothing, wishing he hadn't said anything.

"James, did she?"

"She seemed healthy to me. That's all I'll say." He tries to sugarcoat whatever experience he had with my mom. I scoff. "I just wanted you to know I'm aware that's not why you're back. I want to be here for whatever reason you are. I feel like I owe it to you."

"You're late to the party, James. A lot has happened that you could have been a part of." I cross my arms in front of him. "But you decided to leave, which is okay," I disclaim. "We were young, and you had a career you wanted to pursue. I'm happy it worked out for you, but that's what happens when you walk away from people. You lose the intimate access you once had to them. You miss out."

He hasn't missed out on a damn thing. I'm just saying what sounds good. Saying what sounds better than my truth.

He lifts himself to the left, reaches into his back pocket, and retrieves his wallet. "Here. This is my business card. My cellphone number is listed on the very bottom."

I accept it from him. A professional headshot depicts his pearly smile curved over a nourished beard with his dream job title formatted to the right of it.

"Do you work tomorrow?" James asks.

"Every day starting at 2 p.m."

"Burgers at the diner for lunch. For old-time's sake. At noon?" He pauses before making a promise. "If you don't show, I will leave you alone, but either way, you know where to find me and how to get ahold of me."

He leaves it at that and walks away and back out the door.

I reach my hand to the bump of my stomach and rub it out of a motherly instinct.

I'm slightly disgusted with myself. I am pregnant with a dead man's baby, who I'm being accused of murdering, and now I'm considering a date with an old lover.

I pledge to myself that if I decide to meet up with James tomorrow, I will tell him everything. Where I went, why I moved, and why I came back.

I don't owe him an explanation of my past. In fact, I don't owe that to anybody besides my unborn child, but it seems like the right thing to do.

Also, because of his career as a divorce attorney, it could work in my favor if he's able to provide some level of advice.

Chapter 30

"Ooo-la-la," Lily shimmies her shoulders at what she witnessed. She assumes it's a good thing. "You've caused a lot of traffic since you started working here. It hasn't even been a week! Is that your baby daddy?"

Her question reveals her young age and the gap between her and Tony. I instantly recognize the similarities of our relationships, only this is just the beginning for her.

I glare. "No, and please don't ever ask about that again."

"I'm sorry." Her face droops as if she finally realizes how unexciting this pregnancy is for me.

"Don't be. It's okay." I say, but Lily gives me a moping nod before turning on her heels back to the host stand with guilt for asking. "Hey, wait. I have a question for you."

She spins back around. "What is it?"

"You and Tony were having an... *intense* conversation last night. Are you sure everything is okay?"

Lily's expression illustrates nervousness. She walks back up to the bar, closing the space between us.

"Remember what I told you? About how he doesn't want anyone to find out about us?"

I nod with understanding.

"Okay, well, I guess he said I'm making it too obvious lately."

I won't admit it to her, but I can see why he says that. The way she looks at him, talks about him, and refers to him. It's more than friendly, but it doesn't warrant the way I saw him confronting her about it.

"Can I give you my advice?" I ask for permission because I know how annoying someone's unsolicited two cents can be.

A couple walks through the door and waits to be seated, leaving us little time to discuss further. She looks over her shoulder and then back at me. "I want to hear what you have to say. Make it fast."

I speed through my words. "I don't know what was said, but the way he spoke to you – his finger in your face, his eyes gaping into you like that – it's not okay. You need to be honest with yourself and the people around you about what you go through. Do you understand me?"

She walks backward to the host stand with her usual beatific smile wiped from her face as she acknowledges my words.

"Please be careful," I mouth to her.

—

Although I'm tempted to linger around after I'm expected to, I don't want Tony to know that I see through him after what I witnessed last night.

At the end of my shift, I cash myself out with one hundred and forty dollars in tips and head to the back to gather my things to leave.

Lily is bussing a table, and Tony is in his office working on putting out the next schedule, so I don't have to worry about walking in on another argument.

I take my bag off the hook and glower at Tony through

the window of his office door before leaving. I capture his attention with a knock and plaster on a false smile with a wave goodbye.

If his relationship with Lily is as dangerous as I'm making it out to be, challenging him will only escalate what Lily already puts up with.

She's restocking the glasses behind the bar when I approach her and hand my phone over.

"I think it would be good for us to exchange numbers, Lily."

She sets down the cup in her hand and hesitantly takes the phone from me. I was going to write my number down for her, but I still don't know it by heart.

"Just for work purposes," I say to mollify the underlying reason.

She puts her number in and hands it back to me. "Thanks, Vivian. See you tomorrow?"

"Yep, and every day after that."

I don't think anybody takes a day off at this place.

Chapter 31

Leaving Lily behind at the bar wasn't easy, but exchanging numbers made me feel comfortable enough to go.

I walk back into my hotel feeling content aside from being a suspect in Ezra's murder.

"Excuse me, ma'am!" A front desk agent calls out as I walk through the lobby to the elevator. "Are you the occupant staying in room 512?" The words pass through her bright red lips.

I stop in my tracks but step from side to side, holding back the urge to use the bathroom. Intensifying my need to go is my baby resting right on top of my full bladder.

"Yes. Is everything okay?"

"Unfortunately not. We will be discontinuing your stay for violation of our pet policy. You have until tomorrow at our checkout time of 11 a.m. to vacate your room. A fee of two hundred and fifty dollars will be added to your total."

I squeeze my eyes shut and shake my head with humiliation and a rush of stress. I have been religiously hanging the *do-not-disturb* sign on the door, but I must have forgotten.

Pregnancy brain.

I have nowhere else to go. This was the cheapest rate I could find, and it's right across the street from my job. My eyes shoot back open, and I move toward her.

"I can explain."

"There are no exceptions to the rule," the agent insists.

I smack my lips and swing my bag off my shoulder to dig for my wallet. I grab my night's worth of tips and look around to make sure no one sees what I'm about to do.

"Here, take this. This is one hundred and forty dollars. In exchange for letting me stay and removing the pet violation fee."

"I'm sorry, but I can't accept tips." The agent follows the rules by the book, and it's starting to piss me off. I calm myself down and remind myself she's just doing her job.

"Please! I just moved back to the city because my husband is..." I almost tell her Ezra is dead, but I don't need another person side-eyeing me, especially her, so I tell the same lie I've told several times now. "I'm here caring for my sick mother. I'm pregnant, and staying here allows me to get to and from her house and my job to stay afloat."

I point across the street to Tony's Tap to make my lie more believable.

"I'm sorry for violating the policy, but I need this. Bad," I emphasize and shake the money at her with a raise of my eyebrows.

My bladder feels like it's about to explode, so I wish she would hurry up and take it.

Accepting the cash, she peaks through her peripheral vision and pinches it out of my hand. "Someone else might not be so nice next time. Keep your do-not-disturb sign hung at all times."

My forearm props on the front desk, and my head cradles

into it. With a sigh, I stand back up and thank her profusely.

Apologizing, coaxing, and appreciation will not be enough to see me through my situation. I need to be more careful. Being almost halfway through my pregnancy, there is no room for error.

When I arrive back to my hotel room, I cuddle in bed with Nina and try to quiet my mind.

As tempted as I am to ponder Ezra's death, going to lunch with James tomorrow, followed by a long night of work, will require a night of rest.

I tuck the growing list of possibilities into the nightstand drawer.

Out of sight, out of mind.

Chapter 32

Things still aren't back to normal between Sasha and me since the night we clashed. We text here and there, but our conversations are less exuberant than before. Even so, talking to her will hopefully calm my nerves while I walk to meet James at the diner. I need a leisurely conversation, so I dial her number as I get out of the elevator.

"Hello?" she answers.

"Hey!" I say, pushing my way out of the hotel doors and into the bustling city. "I feel like we haven't spoken in forever. I just wanted to give you a call. You'd never guess who I'm on my way to have lunch with."

I'm trying to force normalcy on us both, but nothing is normal anymore. Everything is different.

"Oh, God. Who?"

"James! He came into my job yesterday and told me he knows I'm not here for my mom. He said he went looking for me last year when he moved back and went to her house as a last resort. According to him, she seems unbothered by the fact that she hasn't seen or heard from her own daughter in a decade."

Sasha sighs with sympathy. "Scratch what I said about ever reaching out to her. That's horrible." She switches topics. "You have enough on your plate right now. How are you doing since the interrogation with that asshole detective?"

"Fine, I guess. I still haven't heard from a woman in the department, as requested. Maybe they listened back to my conversation with Detective Douglas Ranger and decided to let me off the hook."

I turn a corner and can already see the sign to the diner in the distance. The exact aroma of fries and cheese-layered burgers I remember swarms through the air around me.

"Trust me, they aren't done with you." Fervor leaks through Sasha's voice. "I was brought in for questioning not once, not twice, but *three times*! It was frustrating, but I cooperated. You should, too."

"Oh." I pause, feeling anxiety build up inside of me. "I didn't know they were questioning you to that extent. I'll brace myself if that's the case."

I approach the diner, and I can already see James through the window, sitting at a booth, waiting for me eagerly.

I take the last few moments I have left to tell Sasha the critical detail I forgot to mention to her before. I hold the phone to my ear and aim a finger up to James for him to be patient.

"But hey, I've been meaning to tell you this. I left my wedding ring on the kitchen counter, but the detective said they didn't see it anywhere. Isn't that strange?"

Sasha is as stumped as me. "Um, very. What the hell could have happened to it?"

"That's what I'm wondering. Now, the only possibility that makes sense to me is a burglar, but it's hard to say since they aren't disclosing his cause of death or if anything else went missing."

Sasha sighs, taking a load off. "Well, it was announced that his funeral is tomorrow. Maybe more will come out after that."

"Wait. Really?" Plugging my other ear, I make sure I'm hearing her correctly.

James catches my expression. He holds up a thumb to ask *are you alright* through the window. I nod and make an effort to hurry off the phone.

"Okay, listen. He's waiting for me. I have to go, but please go to the funeral tomorrow. I will never ask you for another favor."

"What? Hell no! I'm off the hook. Detectives will surely be there looking for suspicious guests. No, no, and no. I cannot do that. I won't. I have shit to lose," Sasha refuses.

I stomp my foot to the ground.

"Sasha, I need you to do this for me. Listen into conversations, focus on people's body language, tell me who is there... you may be off the hook, but they are still latching onto me like a mad dog."

She lets out a heavy breath. "I'll think about it."

Chapter 33

"Everything alright?" James asks as I frantically slide into the booth across from him.

"Yes, all is good. I'm starving!" I grab hold of one of the menus lying between us. "How long did I keep you waiting?"

"I've been here since 11:45 a.m." He twists his wrist to where a costly watch wraps around. "So a little over thirty minutes."

"Phew," I exaggerate. "Thank you for waiting for me."

"No, thank *you*. For coming."

I smile up at him over the menu, and a server approaches our table with a platter.

"Oh, we still haven't ordered yet. Maybe that's for a different table?" I suggest politely, although I wish I would've accepted the meals. I'm starving.

James reaches across for my hand. "I ordered for us."

I tug away from him and set the menu aside, making room for our combos.

"Here's the double cheeseburger with fries," she announces as she sets the first basket in front of James. "And here's your cheeseburger with extra pickles, fries, and a side of ranch."

My mouth oozes, and my heart softens. He still remembers my order.

Without wasting any time, I dig into my basket for a French fry and dip it into the ranch. I avoid the seriousness of why we're here by asking a question I'm genuinely curious to know.

"So, tell me," I say with a finger covering my mouth of fries, "what's the craziest divorce case you've had?"

He giggles with a full mouth of his burger. "Funny you ask. A case I just closed was by far one of the messiest I've had. My client filed for divorce because she was certain her husband was cheating on her. She put in their marriage contract that in the case of infidelity of any sort, he would have to pay all of her bills for as long as she was alive."

My eyebrows raise, wishing I had thought of that with Ezra.

"To prove he was cheating, we hired a private investigator. Turns out the woman her husband was having an affair with ended up being his very own divorce attorney."

A hand slaps over my mouth, covering my uncontrollable, blaring laugh. "Okay, I was not expecting that!"

We're laughing together now.

"Neither was I, but what happened next was even worse." James' tone grows serious. "Instead of living off of him for the rest of her life, she *killed* him!" His hands go up in the air with misunderstanding. "I mean, why would she do that? So now, instead of living a completely financially free life, freedom is the last thing she has."

My laugh subsides, and my chest grows hot. I need to change the subject before I lose my composure.

"And your dad, Mr. Sterling. How's he been? I'm sure he's proud his son followed in his footsteps."

My question obliterates the smile James just had a moment ago, and now we both look sorrowful. I reach across the table to him, my face puckered with concern.

He sucks food out of his teeth to hold back tears.

"He passed away last year. Prostate cancer." He squeezes the hand I extended to him when he says this. Tears prick my eyes. "That's why I moved back. I took over his firm, Sterling Pierce Law Group."

I shake my head, thinking about how it must have made him feel when I lied to him about my mother being sick. Mr. Sterling was a single father and worked hard. He was the sole provider and caretaker of the household — a rare dynamic. Something I envied but also appreciated.

"James, I am so sorry. How have you been holding it together all this time?"

"I know it sounds cliche, but losing my dad changed the way I see the world. How I look at life. The way I embrace relationships." His eyes flash into mine. "That's why I wanted to see you when I got back. Even though we were young, I never stopped cherishing what we had, Vivian. I'm knocking on thirty's door, yet no woman has ever brought me close to what we had together. Even as teenagers, you were the kind of woman I wished my mother was."

I push the basket of my unfinished food to the center of the table. My appetite is shot. He's saying these things as if he knows what I'm hiding from him. It must be a sign.

"James, I need to talk to you about something."

He imitates me, pushing his food off to the side, too. He leans closer, giving me his undivided attention.

"I'm listening."

"You know now that I didn't come here for my mom."

He acknowledges that with a non-judgmental expression.

"Well, the truth is, after graduation, I packed up and moved to Denver. I got a full-ride scholarship. My mom had no idea.

The money you used to hold for me so she wouldn't steal it is what helped me buy the car I used to drive myself cross-country. I didn't tell her anything."

"Understandably so," he acknowledges.

His responses are bland and concise, letting me know he's all ears.

I bite my tongue as I try to find the words for the rest of what I want James to know.

I look out the window as if it will reflect the courage I need to continue. Instead, the reflection of a recognizable woman takes me out of our conversation.

Her face transports me back to when Detective Douglas Ranger picked me up and brought me to the station. In his car, a photo rested in the glint of the overhead light in the front seat.

Detective Kelly Ranger. Together for thirty-two years and counting. She's the love of my life.

His voice rings through my imagination when my eyes make contact with hers.

I wasn't referring to his *wife* when I requested to speak with a woman!

"Excuse me, I need to use the restroom," I say to James, excusing myself from the table.

James' voice grows quiet while I walk away from the table as he speaks.

"Wait! Vivian! What's going on?"

I lock myself into the single-stall bathroom. He can't find out about everything, not like this.

Chapter 34

I was hoping James and Detective Kelly Ranger would have left by now so I could dodge the bullet of explaining myself to either of them.

To my dismay, James has been calling my name from the other side of the bathroom door. It's been almost an hour, and he's losing his patience, although I wish he would run out of it so I don't have to face him, but after this long, I know he isn't leaving anytime soon.

Before this situation gets any worse than it already is, I walk out of the bathroom.

James is eye-to-eye with me immediately. He tells me Detective Kelly Ranger sat with him and told him everything.

"Everything?" I ask with mortification. She is just as malicious as her husband to have stolen my spot at the table and given him the rundown on me.

"EVERYTHING! You didn't think what the detective told me would have been good information for me to know? I have been keeping up with you for the past week now. I'm a divorce attorney, for Christ's sake! I already had a murderous client, and now I'm sitting here having lunch with someone suspected of murdering her husband, too. Do you know what this can do to my reputation?"

My emotions go from anxious to livid in a matter of seconds.

"I was going to tell you! Let me explain, James. I can make everything make sense."

"I don't think you can. Getting back in contact with you may have been a mistake. I'm sorry for making you feel pressured to come to lunch today, but we're done here."

I grab hold of his arm, but he pulls it away and storms out of the diner, leaving me humiliated as a crowd has formed around us.

"Fuck off!" I yell at the congregation of diner guests staring at me.

Half of them scramble away, and the other half look even more intrigued as I push through them to leave.

By now, I need to go to work, and I'm not even sure how I'll be able to concentrate after what just happened.

My phone dings with a text.

Lily: Comin' in today?

Me: Yes. On my way. Sorry for running late.

By the time I get to work, I'm early enough to be taken seriously but late enough for this to be out of character. I walk straight to Tony's office to ensure I'm in no trouble.

"Oh, Bozzelli, you have nothing to worry about as long as it doesn't become a habit," he warns me.

I let him slide by addressing me by my last name this time.

"I'll make sure it doesn't happen again."

I tried to assure him as credibly as I could, but today was out of my control. With Ezra's murder being unsolved, I don't know when I'll ever have a grip on anything at all.

At least at the bar, I feel a sense of domination. As much of a control freak as Tony can be, he is far from a micro-manager. As long as customers are happy and he's making money, he trusts us.

For the rest of the night, I am occupied by a slew of customers. It's busy enough that my mind barely has a chance to wander off to think about Ezra, James, or detectives. I'm beginning to come to terms with the thought of becoming a mother, so I let those thoughts linger.

Chapter 35

I sit up straight in bed, jolted awake by a call from Sasha. I hate that whenever the phone rings, I still have irrational thoughts that it could be Ezra calling.

It sends me into a panic until I remember he's dead.

I slept so long it's already nearing my 2 p.m. shift at the bar today.

The morning sun seeps through the hotel curtains as I ready myself for drama in place of continental breakfast served in the hotel lobby.

"Tell me everything," I demand.

Sasha went to the funeral as I begged her to. She allows me to decide how upset I want to feel after this.

"Are you sure you want me to go into detail?"

"I want to know every detail, no matter how unimportant it seems to you."

She exhales under pressure. "I'll start from the beginning, but you're not going to like it, so prepare yourself." The sound of Sasha's fingers tapping her phone comes through my speaker. "Look at the picture I just sent to you."

My heart throbs with difficulty as if thick blood pumps through me, making it hard for me to breathe. Shining through my screen is a picture of the silver sedan in the church parking lot where the funeral was held.

Claire Bluff's husband is stepping out of the driver's side. On the passenger side, a large, black hat rests on Claire's head. She's wearing a black and somber dress, and her eyes are hidden behind a black pair of sunglasses as if she is preparing herself to shed a river of tears.

Her husband trails behind her like a damn puppy, oblivious to her adultery. I guess men really don't have the other-worldly intuition we do as women.

"That bitch!" I yell into the phone. Nina's ears flinch in my direction as she lays in my lap, sensing my hostility.

Sasha pauses, allowing me time to process what I see.

"How did she muster up the audacity to drop my husband off drunk like that?"

"Don't be mad at me when I say this, but Vivian, you can't blame her. Ezra let this happen. When her husband finds out about their affair, which he will, she will get what she deserves. But honestly, you don't even know what was going on for certain. You don't have proof. Maybe you're overthinking the whole thing."

Sasha's level-headed response sinks into me like a set of fangs. While she could be right, I don't want to accept it. I won't. The situation with Claire has made it easier to stuff grief into a sinkhole and hate Ezra even more.

Since her husband was driving the silver sedan in the photo, it could also make sense that he dropped Ezra off that night. I'm okay with either possibility, but I'm not letting it go altogether.

Gently picking Nina up off my lap and setting her on the bed, I stand to my feet and pace from wall to wall.

"Alright, that's all I needed to know. Thank you for doing that for me."

I feel a sense of relief and closure. An assumption that crawled through my mind and created narratives like a spider in its cobweb, multiplying its threads, is now fulfilled with a cross between a possible truth I knew from the very beginning. Or maybe a new suspect who was outside our home just hours before Ezra's murder.

"Hold on, I wasn't done. There's more," Sasha insists to continue.

"I said that's all I need to know."

Sasha usually does what she wants anyway, but for whatever reason, she lays off and ends our conversation without a fight.

I locate the piece of scribbled paper in the nightstand and drag my finger down the page until I find where I circled the words, *silver sedan*.

Next to it, I draw a sharp star.

Chapter 36

"You seem much happier today," Lily observes.

I get slightly defensive at her comment.

"Are you saying I'm usually in a bad mood?" I pretend not to know what she's talking about, but even after a horrifying lunch with James the other day, I can't help but feel elated.

Sasha confirming my hunch about Claire Bluff and giving me someone else to pin Ezra's death on might take the heat off me.

"No, you're just," she pauses to think, "glowing and cheerful. You know what they say about a pregnant woman that's glowing!"

"Um, no, I don't. How does it go?" I don't know the first thing about pregnancy. I've been rolling with the punches since day one, so I'm intrigued by Lily's comment, even if it's an unreliable myth.

"A pregnant woman with glowing skin is usually expecting a boy. Girls suck the life out of you. It's just one of those old wives tales." She dismisses it, but I take it seriously.

I bring a hand to my face to feel the softness. Contrary to what my doctor told me, the morning sickness has eased off over the last several days. Maybe Lily is onto something.

"While it's slow, let's test it out," she suggests.

We've been sitting at the bar together for hours, waiting for a customer to walk through the doors. She reaches her hands around the back of her neck and unclasps a necklace with a dolphin pendant.

"Hold out your hand," she insists with a smile stretched across her face. A left dimple appears. I've never noticed it before.

"What are you doing?"

"When do you find out the gender?" she questions as though she's giving me an ultimatum.

"I'm about seventeen weeks now, so I have another three weeks to go until my next appointment. That's when I should find out."

She shakes her head as if I'm wrong. "Yeah, I can't wait that long." Lily holds the necklace still before letting it go and allowing it to dangle over my palm. "If it moves in circles, that means it's going to be a girl. If it motions back and forth, then I'm right. You'll be giving me a nephew."

I chuckle at her comment a little too hard, and my hand touches the necklace. "Stop, don't move." Lily halts the chain midair with her hand before releasing it again and scrutinizing its sway for several seconds.

Her forehead wrinkles, and her mouth opens with a grin so big I can almost see every one of her teeth. The exhilaration she has for my pregnancy makes me feel the pleasures of motherhood for once.

"It's a boy!" She yells so loud I cover her mouth, hoping nobody caught that. "I was right!"

As if on queue, Tony pushes his way through the door from the kitchen. "Lily isn't very good at keeping secrets." He chimes in nonchalantly as if he were a part of our conversation. He keeps walking past us toward the entrance door. I stare at him blankly.

Lily's excitement plummets into the base of her stomach. I know that feeling all too well.

Tony opens the door at the front entrance and hangs a sign on the back of it. Without making my concern obvious, I give Lily a backing stare.

"Vivian, you can head out for the day." The slamming sound of the door behind Tony ends his sentence.

"Wait a minute. It's only six o'clock," I object. "There's still an entire night ahead. What if it picks up?"

He passes us on his way back to his office without even looking in our direction once. "It won't because I just hung a *closed* sign. Lily and I can close the house. Go home, Vivian. Oh, and congratulations." Tony disappears into the back, and I wait for the vibration of his office door closing before saying anything.

Lily avoids looking at my face as I speak. "Are you sure you're okay?"

When a nod of her head replaces her usual assuring chirps, I take that as a telling answer.

"I'm not leaving."

My words send her gaze to snap at me. "You have to! You're only going to make it worse."

Lily may be young and naive, but I have to admit she's right.

"I feel wrong to leave you here. It makes me nervous."

"Why do you care so much?" Lily's question catches me off guard. It brings me back to why I always wondered the same thing about Sasha. "I promised to keep your secret, and I ruined it. I'm so stupid."

"Don't talk about yourself like that. And who cares that he

knows? Remember, I was only hiding it to get the job. I'm in the door now! It doesn't matter who knows anymore." Although I say this so she can forgive herself, I'm also reassuring myself in the same breath. "Don't worry about it."

One side of her mouth goes up into a slight grin. "I'll text you if I need anything. You're just across the street," Lily assures me.

Surprised by how she knows where I've been living, I have to ask. "How would you know that I stay across the street?"

She gives me a *duh* look. "You must agree that I'm stupid if you don't think I see you walk to and from the hotel every day. I can see it from here."

Now *I* want to tell myself I'm stupid.

To avoid making matters worse, I leave Tony and Lily alone for the rest of the night, feeling comfortable that I'm just a call and a crosswalk away.

Chapter 37

As much as I didn't want to leave Lily at the bar with Tony, it felt good to have gotten out of there early. I have the rest of the evening to relax for the first time in a while.

A lot has surfaced in such little time, so my body and baby could use the extra rest.

The front desk agent who cut me slack for having Nina in my room in exchange for a night's worth of tips gives me a welcoming nod at my arrival through the lobby.

Her mouth doesn't move, yet a strong, feminine voice crawls through the drums of my ears.

"Vivian Bozzelli?"

Slow on my heels, I rotate my body in the direction of Detective Kelly Ranger.

I side-eye the front desk agent and then proceed to talk out the side of my mouth so she doesn't have more of a reason to look at me like a problematic guest.

"What do you want now?"

"You know what we want. You know what I'm here for. I need you to tell me the truth about your husband." Her tone is persuasive.

"Claire Bluff. She and her husband. Look into them if you

haven't already." I'm confident in this suggestion after what I saw.

"And why would we do that?" She protests.

"The night my husband died, he was dropped off by a silver car, and I believe it belongs to them."

"We'll look into it, but we still need you to cooperate."

My chest grows hot, and so does the rest of my body at her comment. It seems like nothing I say or do will help my case.

"Leave me the hell alone, Detective. I have contributed to your lousy investigation with every piece of information I could have given you. I refuse to say another word until I know my husband's cause of death. In the meantime, it would be appreciated if you all would stop showing up to my job, crashing in on my personal time, and coming to where I live."

Her eyes scan the hotel lobby in judgment of my living situation.

"Hm, and as in personal time, are you referring to the date you were on just weeks after your husband's death?"

A dragon-like sigh exits through my nose with a huff. James hasn't responded to my calls or texts. He hasn't lingered in my shadows since she took away my chance to tell him everything myself.

"Our team is still waiting on the autopsy report. Even escalating the process can take several weeks. This could be a closed case if you would tell us what happened that night."

"By the time he was dead, I was gone. Okay? What don't you guys understand?"

Unable to hold my composure any longer, the decibel of my voice loses control. I stick my finger into her face like her husband did to me. I drill it toward her to emphasize my words.

"This is the problem with our justice system." My voice shakes. "You guys want to take the easiest course of resistance by pinning the murder of a man on his wife because you know a naive jury will eat it up and then spit me out into a prison cell for the rest of my innocent life. Then what happens to my child? Because you guys aren't going to look after them. They'll be another number in foster care. So I suggest you do your job and do it thoroughly, or you will never close this case. Not as long as you point your fingers at me." I step closer to her. "No pun intended."

My eyes rolled over her with repulsion before turning to resume my walk to the elevator. Anger smolders through me, clogging my lungs with anger.

The elevator dings at its landing. It slides open, inviting my thoughts and me inside.

The justice system is the government's corrupt version of sororities and fraternities. Individuals under oath slither in tandem through society like snakes disguised as heroes with badges instead of capes. Loopholes gape deep into the already fundamentally screwed-up system. The system that turned a blind eye to my abusive husband is the same one sticking a pin through me and onto their bulletin board of suspects for his murder.

Chapter 38

Twenty weeks, twenty weeks left to go until my due date.

Me: You were right.

I send a text to Lily to confirm her old wives' tales were spot on as the ultrasound tech wipes away the gel from my stomach.

Lily: lksdhflngwesflk

Me: Huh?

Lily: Ur so old.

I guess the younger generations type a slew of random letters as if they've just had a brain aneurysm to express their uncontrollable emotions.

"Congratulations. I'm a mom of a little boy, too. They're wild, and it isn't always easy, but it's the best thing I've ever done." The tech encourages me softly with a smile of sympathy.

This tech also did my first ultrasound, so with no mention of a baby's father, I think she realizes by now that I'm doing this alone. It seems like it gives her an inclination to drop words of wisdom and encouragement, and I appreciate it more than she knows.

Coming to my pregnancy checkups alone is one of the most isolating yet reality-checking experiences.

"He looks perfectly healthy," she assures me. "We'll see you in four weeks."

I thank her and exit down the hall to the lobby, or at least in the direction I think it is.

I bend around corner after corner as if trapped in a maze when I bump recklessly and by accident into another woman.

"I'm so sorry!" With a deep apology, I hold out my hand to another pregnant stomach, and the woman's hair brushes against it. Her startled face is pierced with a mole on the right side.

I instantly recognize her as the woman who stood in front of me in line at my first appointment. Her bump has popped even more since I saw her then. If I had to guess, her due date is right around the corner.

"Excuse me," she says, adjusting her cross-body purse around her bump. The woman steps around me, avoiding an interaction as long as our last.

"Wait, do you know how to get out of here?" I ask. She stops and looks back at me. I widen my eyes, breathing heavily. "I've been walking around forever trying to find the exit. It's so confusing!"

She beats around my small talk. "Um, sure. This way." The woman keeps it short with me. I can tell she doesn't want to walk and talk, so we don't. Besides, it would be a little invasive to strike up a conversation with a random lady in a clinic and ask what her story is.

I can't help that I picked up on her sadness before, and I'm picking up on it again today.

Regardless if I wanted to talk to her, she gave me no way in any way. She picks up momentum when we reach the lobby, leaving me too far behind to keep up.

Captivated by her eagerness to be unseen, my eyes latch onto her from an unnoticeable distance. I glue my phone to the side of my face as though I'm on a phone call while going in the opposite direction of the train station.

I blend in with a group of people for another block or so until she stops at the passenger side of a black car. As if I'm taking cover in a call of duty, I stand between the indent of a coffee shop and an art studio.

Watching her. Watching the car.

Why is she just... standing there? I think to myself. But as I observe the situation a bit longer, my eyes squint at the left bumper. A *dented* left bumper.

I take my phone away from my face and navigate to my camera.

Detective Douglas Ranger enters the frame from the other side of the car, looking equally as suspicious as the woman.

Snap. Snap.

He opens the passenger side door and rests his hand on her lower back to assist her into the car.

Snap.

Rather than watching her step, his head selfishly turns in every direction, including mine. I have to dip back in between the walls of the building.

He monitors his surroundings before nearly shutting the door on her leg and walking to the other side of the car. He pulls away discreetly, so he thinks.

If this is what it looks like, I may have just found my way into a love triangle and out of Ezra's murder case.

Chapter 39

Lily is over the moon that I'm having a boy. "Oh, my God! He just kicked my hand! What does that feel like?!"

"Like bubbles blowing and then bursting. Over and over again." That was the best way I could describe it. Between Lily's bliss and finally feeling him kick the past few weeks my heart feels full lately.

I've gotten three paychecks, enough to show proof of income for an apartment. My tips have been keeping me afloat to stay in the hotel. I still don't know how she could afford it, but Sasha sent me a few thousand dollars for an apartment security deposit so I can live with normalcy again. Lily started washing my clothes for me when she realized I was wearing the ones I had repeatedly.

It presumably takes a village, as the saying goes.

In the back of my mind is a weapon I have been preparing to use if something, or anyone, tries to ruin this.

"Alright, I'm going to get going."

We finally hired another bartender, so my shifts have been shorter, allowing me more time to run errands. Today's is an apartment showing.

"I'll let you know how it goes."

I pry myself out of the bar stool my body has sunk into, leaving its mark. The simplest movements have become difficult as I get closer to thirty weeks into my pregnancy.

"Hold on!" Lily grabs my stomach with both hands and leans down, placing a kiss above my belly button. "Bye, Baby Reese."

"That's not going to be his name," I snort at Lily's continued attempt to talk me into her baby name ideas.

She stands straight, and our eyes meet with her hands still fixated on my bump. "Come on. You hated Beck. You despised Oslo, and now you don't like Reese. You hate my ideas!"

Lily lacks emotional control, but I remind myself how young she is.

"Don't be dramatic. I never said I hated any of your ideas. I actually don't mind Reese, but I think I'll have to see his face before deciding on a name."

Her hands fall from my stomach, longing against her sides with a hunched back and sad lips. "That's too far away!" she complains.

I pull her in for a tight squeeze. "It'll come faster than you think." I pat her back a couple of times before releasing our hug and walking around her. "I can't be late. I'll see you tomorrow!"

—

On my walk to the train station to go to the apartment showing, my face is in my phone, staring at the doubtful texts from Sasha.

Sasha: Could it be his daughter?

Me: That's not what it looked like to me. Can't think about this right now. Headed to the showing. I'll let you know

how it goes. Thanks for making this possible.

Sasha seems to think the woman I saw with Detective Douglas Ranger was a family member or someone with a more platonic relationship. Her logic was, *why would he use his work vehicle to drive his pregnant mistress to her doctor's appointment?*

My logic is, *why not?* He's a detective, which translates to a manipulator.

If he's anything like the ones I've seen on reality TV, he can talk an innocent person into unknowingly admitting they committed a crime. Or bribe someone into snitching on their friend with a reward of a fast food combo. If he'll do that, why wouldn't he drive his mistress around in his work vehicle? It's less suspicious.

I tap away from my text string with Sasha and into the ignored one with James. I start drafting a message.

I've texted him countless times since Detective Kelly Ranger threw a wrench in our date. I've called him and left voicemails. I've tried everything.

After typing and deleting words several times, I erase my thoughts altogether and stop typing. It's stupid of me to keep trying. He's obviously not over it since I haven't heard back from him.

Then, I think maybe he is.

Three dots appear at the bottom of our conversation. He's responding.

I swipe out of our messages so he doesn't see that after weeks, I was miraculously drafting something at the very moment he was, too.

James Pierce: Hey. Hope you and the baby are doing okay.

You deserve an apology. In person. Also, I think I know...

The rest of the text is cut off.

As much as I want to open it to see what else he said and what he knows, I can't let him know how eager I've been to hear from him. Since everything happened, I wished I hadn't pushed him away. It would've given me the upper hand to be forthcoming sooner, before Detective Kelly.

Distracting me from the urge to respond is an announcement of my stop on the overhead speaker of the train. I step off and start in the direction of the apartment building — our future home. Hopefully.

A part of me feels worthless to be struggling as badly as I am.

At the same time, when I lived in society's idea of abundance — the house, the car, the husband, the money — I was in misery.

Ground zero.

Rock bottom.

The silver lining is that I can go up from here, even if that means starting in a shitty, overpriced apartment.

Chapter 40

Photographers sure do a good job of taking pictures of real estate. I don't know what I expected to see from the cheapest apartment listing I could find.

Loose panels of wood creak under each step to the second level of the complex. Baby boy seems to tuck himself right up against my lungs, making it difficult to catch a breath.

The property manager jingles a ring of keys as we approach the apartment door of the unit of my interest. "No pets allowed. No smoking. Utilities are included. There is no in-unit laundry, but the washroom is on the first floor."

As I nod at the information, the door presses open from his forceful entry as if it were glued closed. There is a strong stench of mildew that spills from inside the apartment.

"What's that smell?"

"Oh, it's just the carpet. Don't worry about that; it will be replaced before you move in."

Hiding the scrunch of my nose, I imagine myself and a newborn baby living here. The combination of postpartum and stairs will make laundry on the first floor feel a mile away.

"Are there any units on the first floor available?"

"Those units come with a complementary garage, so for three hundred dollars more, yes. Otherwise, we have apartments on the third floor-"

It's slightly rude of me, but I cut him short. "Oh, no thanks. This will do." *But will it?* I think to myself, my mind flashing back to the palatial home I left with Ezra.

For the first time in a while, my thoughts wander off into how much easier and comfortable it would've been to stay. Could the financial freedom, nannies, housekeepers, and simply a home I could call mine have overshadowed the treacherousness of our marriage?

Of course not. I would smack myself if I were alone right now.

"So, what do you think of the place?" the property manager asks, startling me out of my imagination.

I nod with strained approval. "I think it's home." Those loose panels of wood creak under my uncertain words.

I walk to the far window of the living room and split the blinds with two fingers to see what view I'd have from here. It's nothing exciting. Just a parking lot of outdated, rusted cars planted in their assigned spots, malnourished grass and trees, and a big ugly dumpster for tenants to swing their trash into.

Although it's far from orderly and uniform, something seems out of place. Too good to be here.

Like a piece to a puzzle in the wrong spot, a shiny black car that is nicer than all the rest is squeezed between the dumpster and a set of garages to the right of it.

A dented left bumper reveals itself.

"Everything alright?" the property manager asks me from behind as he notices the defensive shift in my body language.

"Um." I slide my phone out of my back pocket, one hand still holding the blinds open while I check the time with the other.

I'm tempted to open the unread message from James. But now is not the time.

"I lost track of time, and I need to be somewhere. Is there an online application I can submit?"

"Yes, I can send it to your email. Unless you have any other questions, I can walk you back down."

But I'm already out of the apartment and creaking down the flight of stairs.

I gather my bearings to come face-to-face with Detective Douglas Ranger for what I hope is the last time he has the arrogance to hold me accountable for Ezra's death.

Chapter 41

My knuckles feel like they'll be bruised after how hard I knocked on Detective Douglas Ranger's car window. I interrupt his lunch of a chili dog. He plops it down onto the tinfoil in his lap.

"Step away from the door, Vivian." His voice is muffled behind the glass as I back away.

He gets out and leans the back of his body against the car. His arms cross over his stomach while using his tongue to get leftover food between his gums.

Gross.

I don't waste another moment to defy his attempt at cornering me into confessing to something I didn't do. I didn't want the apartment anyway, but he could have ruined this opportunity for me if the property manager had seen him.

"I made it clear to your wife that until my husband's cause of death has been found, you guys will not get another word out of me."

Detective Douglas doesn't let up. "This is your last chance to be cooperative with us. Otherwise, we'll have to take a more aggressive force of action against you. Do you understand?"

I move toward him too close for comfort.

"Oh, I don't think *you* understand. I'll talk if you want me to talk. You're going to wish I shut the hell up."

His head tilts parallel to his shoulder. His arms tug tighter around each other as if he's nervous about what I have to say.

He should be.

The information I've been withholding until just the right moment is about to support my case and concurrently go against his investigation.

After navigating to my camera roll, I press the photo of him and the pregnant woman from the clinic into his face.

"What do you want me to say about this?" I press it closer, giving him a better look at his intimate hand on the pregnant woman's back as she gets into his car. "Do you still want me to talk? Or can we call it even?"

For a moment, I doubted myself and thought maybe Sasha was right. This could be anyone – a sister, a daughter. But my rest is assured when his arms slowly untuck from each other, and a bullet of sweat appears on his temple.

"I would love to know what your wife would think of this."

I put him on a timeline in retaliation. He clenches his teeth, and the structure of his jaw protrudes.

"You have until tomorrow morning to remove me as a suspect in this case, or I will make sure that not only Detective Kelly Ranger but every last one of your colleagues knows that you have a child on the way with a woman who is not your wife." I take a look at the photo on the screen for myself. "Because that is *definitely* not her."

I mean this in the most disrespectful way possible. I could see how Douglas and Kelly have become one, but I don't understand how that beautiful woman got past *hello* with him.

A part of me thinks the only way it was possible was if he forced it. I feel disturbed by this assumption.

He still hasn't said another word, and I realize he's not going to. Detective Douglas jumps back into the driver's seat and pulls out of the apartment parking lot.

Feeling satisfied, I watch him screech away and nearly clip another car as he makes his way into the street.

I spin to see if anyone was around to witness my encounter.

An older woman is looking at me through a third-story window of the apartment building. She has the face of a deflated balloon – scrunched up, wrinkled, and sagging, nothing like sweet Ms. Joyce.

While Ms. Joyce looked out for me, this woman looks like she would put a knife in my back and twist it for pleasure, especially after what she just witnessed.

Also, if the apartment layout is as I imagine, she would live directly above me.

At that, I leave and decide against ever stepping back into the vicinity of this apartment ever again.

Chapter 42

"Do you have any idea what he could have meant by that?"

I called Sasha when I got to my hotel. She digs deeper into the text I finally opened from James.

He said he thinks he knows of a way to help me.

I could articulate this in different ways, one being he can get me out of the woods of the murder investigation. If that's the case, I already got it covered. At least, I think so.

"I don't know, but he's a divorce attorney. It could mean anything."

Nina slides against my stomach with the muzzle of her head. I think she somehow senses the baby already.

"Another man with a big title, I see. Maybe now that you have Detective Douglas Ranger off your back, you don't need James anyway."

I forgive Sasha for her ignorance, but James is far from anything like Ezra. The only thing they have in common is a tax bracket.

Freeing me of a response to her comment is an incoming call from James.

"Sasha! He's calling. I'll talk to you later! Okay?" Before she can even say anything, I abandon her on the other line.

"Vivian."

The sound of him saying my name makes my body tingle with arousal. Nina's ears perk up at his voice through the phone as if she remembers it.

"Yes?" I hide my hunger for this conversation behind an attitude.

"I know it's short notice, but can we meet up tonight? Maybe in private this time?"

I laugh off his paranoia. "Where?"

Looking around my hotel room, I know he won't suggest coming here.

"If you feel comfortable with it, we could go to my office?" He's reluctant yet simultaneously welcoming.

My eyes go wide at his suggestion. "If I'm comfortable with it? I think the question is more so if *you're* comfortable with it. I'm a possible murderer, remember? Or have you found a way to get me out of this?"

"Stop," he insists, "I didn't find a way to get you out of anything because there's nothing to get you out of. I know you would never do something like that."

"What did you mean when you said you could help me then? This doesn't sound like anything we can't talk about over the phone."

I don't know why I'm being stubborn. I want to see him. I should act like it.

Frustration laces his voice. "Vivian, I want to see you. Okay? I owe you an apology, but more than that, *yes,* I can help you out of your situation because it's no way to raise a child!"

I become defensive at him for thinking I'm incapable.

"I can do this on my own. I'm doing everything I can to make it possible."

"Not everything. You don't understand!" I hear the clinking of a set of keys in the background. "I'll be there to get you in thirty minutes. Please don't make this harder than it already is."

I feel deplorable at how easy it was for me to give in as I lifted myself off the bed, already slipping on my shoes for him to pick me up.

Chapter 43

I expected nothing short of superb. The swanky theme suits him perfectly, making me feel inferior.

James welcomes me into his office, which consists of ebony wood entirely. The walls are garnished with books. A sumptuous Persian rug hides the wooden floor. His desk is topped with a globe.

A large window shows a view of the street at ground level, so the first thing he does is lower the blinds for apparent reasons.

I look haggard in the same clothes I've been rotating in and out of, which hardly stretch over my pregnant stomach that James can't seem to take his eyes off.

"Here, have a seat."

Since picking me up from the hotel, he hasn't stopped treating me with delicacy. He rolls out a plush-looking chair that I feel like I'm contaminating as I lower myself onto it.

James sits across from me. Separating us is the antique desk with a stack of papers in the middle of it.

"I feel like one of your clients or something," I joke, tucking my hair behind an ear, but James doesn't look in the mood to laugh.

His eyes roll over me with humility and repentance before he shifts into a professional mode. He spreads the stacked documents across the desk.

I'm perplexed.

"What's happening? What is all of this?"

"I'm apologizing to you in the best way I know how."

James positions the last piece of paper to face me and crosses his hands in front of his chest on the desk.

"You're set for life, Vivian."

My eyes scan the documents, and it takes several moments for me to register what I'm looking at. Insurance policy after insurance policy. Retirement and investment accounts. Laying out in front of me is what looks to be an entire estate settlement.

"Whoever you married left you quite the estate. And from the sounds of it, he owed it to you. Every last penny."

I think it pained him to say that.

"James," I express his name with amazement, "how were you able to get all of this in order and do it so quickly?"

"My dad was well-connected. Since taking over Sterling Pierce Law Group, I've gained access to people and resources in high places. Anything is possible."

Apparently so, I think to myself.

"This is. . . impressive."

"I couldn't get myself to reach back out after. . ." he clears his throat, "after what happened, but I knew that when I did, I needed to be able to make it up to you." He steals my hands from the documents, holding them with commitment. "This will take some time to sort out, but if you're patient enough to work with me, I promise the outcome will be in your best interest."

I squeeze his hands in mine to say *thank you*, which is in sync with the squeal of a vehicle braking at the curb and a glint of headlights outside the blind-concealed window.

Our eyes dart to meet each other — mine fearful, his relaxed.

"Calm down. It may just be one of my business partners," James attempts to comfort me.

"On a Sunday at this time of night?" I question.

"Our job never stops." He scoots himself away and stands to his feet. "Stay here."

My stomach clenches. I feel like a secret when he shuts the door behind him and leaves me here. Unable to make out any words, the vibration of his voice trickles down the hallway and overlaps with the voice of a woman.

A woman.

Jealousy plagues me unreasonably as I creep to the door and place my ear to it to get a better seat to whatever conversation is being had.

Words become clearer.

Vivian.

Autopsy.

I know she's here.

Before I realize what I've done, the door to his office crashes closed behind me, and I'm waddling down the hall to where their voices are coming from.

Detective Kelly Ranger stands with James, and my anger bursts out of me.

"I told you guys to leave me the hell alone!" I yell down the hall.

James holds out a hand to me as I charge toward them. "Vivian! Stop!" I continue anyway until all three of us are coalesced into a pod.

"But since you want me to talk so damn bad, here, I'll tell you something you wish-"

"Vivian, I suggest you listen to what I have to say." Detective

Kelly weaves her fingers through one another with poise. "We have the autopsy report for your husband, Ezra Bozzelli." I think the word *husband* bothers James as his nostrils flare. "He passed from carbon monoxide poisoning, and his death is being ruled a suicide."

Surprised by not only his cause of death but the impeccable timing of it being discovered, I question her integrity.

"I spoke to your husband, Detective Douglas, just hours ago, and he didn't have the results. Now they just conveniently come out of the woodwork like this?"

She gives me a mischievous smile. "The truth is, we've had it for weeks. Whatever information you provided must have been good enough for my husband to let you off the hook. I can't make sense of it, but I trust him."

A laugh of ridicule escapes me at her faith in her husband. James looks confused at my reaction.

Detective Kelly Ranger turns her back to us to leave, but I stop her in her tracks before it's too late.

"Wait. Detective, before you go, did you ever look into Claire Bluff or her husband?"

She turns to us with a stumped expression. "You know. We thought we were getting somewhere with that, but nothing came of it. Thanks for the tip, though. Anything else you have to say, Vivian?"

I look at James and back at Detective Kelly.

"Actually, if you have a minute, yes. I do have something else I'd like to tell you."

Detective Kelly Ranger is captivated as I pull my phone out of my pocket and navigate to my camera roll.

Chapter 44

Two years later

"You look beautiful, baby," James says with a hand wrapped tightly around my waist, pulling me in for a peck on the lips.

He's been waiting on me patiently for the last half hour while I finished getting ready for our first-anniversary dinner.

"We'll be back no later than midnight," I say while looping an earring through my earlobe and touching up my lipstick. "Call us if you need anything!"

"Sterling, say *bye, mommy and daddy*!" Lily instructs as she holds him up on her hip, waving at us in illustration.

"Thank you so much for watching him, Lily."

She pinches Sterling's cheek, sending him into laughter. "Watching this little cutie pie is a favor for a favor." I stare at them in adoration, thankful he looks everything like me and nothing like his father.

"Alright, we're going to be late for our reservation," James respectfully rushes me.

My heels knock on the marble tile to meet him at the front entryway.

As James pulls the Porsche out of our horseshoe driveway,

he lays a hand on my thigh, keeping it there for the entirety of the way to the restaurant.

"We have a seven o'clock reservation for the Pierce's," James informs the host.

My stomach flips with butterflies at the sound of *Pierce*'s.

The final string attached to Ezra was a last name I couldn't stand, but in turn, a maiden name that meant nothing to me from a mother I still have yet to rekindle a relationship with.

After collecting money from insurance policies, retirement plans, investment accounts, the warranty from my stolen/lost wedding ring (I truly couldn't figure out what happened to it), and the proceeds from the house we bought together, James loved me even more despite all the mess. Enough to not only marry me but take in Sterling as his own.

At that point, it felt right that I name him in homage to James' father, Mr. Sterling.

Lily felt let down for not having the honor of naming him, but I was focused on far more important things.

It was my idea to hire her as our nanny. The intention was selfish in the sense that I didn't feel comfortable sending Sterling to daycare and wanted to stay far from the stay-at-home mom lifestyle that Ezra would have demanded.

My motive was otherwise entirely selfless for Lily's sake.

Paying far beyond her wage at Tony's Tap, she quit her job at the host stand. It was evidently catastrophic, as the bar shut down six months later. That's what Tony deserved after I walked in on his hand gripped around Lily's neck, later claiming it was her sexual preference. The cry for help in her eyes spoke the same language as mine once did.

I never understood Sasha's determination to help me. After this first-hand experience with Lily, her reasoning was apparent.

"Cheers to another year of true love, making up for lost time, creating memories, navigating parenthood together, and expanding Sterling Pierce Law Group." James initiates a tribute to our first year of marriage with a clank of our champagne glasses.

We have immense plans to grow the law firm into a space for men and women to sever themselves from abusive marriages safely.

James offered me the opportunity to finally put my Political Science degree into use as a Cultural Awareness Director under my one condition of being part-owner of the firm.

If there's one thing my first marriage taught me, it is to never allow a man to dangle control over my head without collateral damage accessible at my fingertips.

That's where I went wrong with Ezra. No matter where I stashed secrets or the lies that I tried to tell, he had the upper hand to always find a way to get his hands on the truth, even if that meant reaching his insolent hands behind the back of a toilet tank.

I don't know how he managed to figure that one out.

Before selling the home as part of the estate settlement process, it was completely cleared and cleaned for newcomers. While the back of a toilet tank would be a strange place for anyone to look, I thought I would do my due diligence and clear that, too.

The pregnancy test box was pretty much nonexistent, and the test lines had faded in color on the stick.

Lying submerged at the very bottom of the tank was my phone. The phone Ezra took from me and never gave back.

You can think you paved your way out of a situation unscathed, but destiny has a special way of finding you and sending a disturbing chill to slither up your spine, vertebrae by vertebrae.

Sometimes, I wish I had done it. Instead of tossing the gun into a random appliance box, I should have used it how he probably planned to.

If only I could rewind time because if I could, I would cuff him to our bed frame by his ankles and wrists. Not one set of cuffs, but two, just in case he got out of the first pair.

Leaving him out of reach to help himself to a phone or any form of communication to call for help, I would have abandoned him long enough until he lusted over the simple thought of water so profoundly that another woman wouldn't have held any level of importance to cross his mind.

The idea of raising another fist to me would have gone to dust with his last breath.

Notice how my pursuit wouldn't have been an instantaneous form of death but rather slow and calculated. Purposefully and by design. It's kind of like stabbing the knife and taking it back out – the damage is done, yet multiplied and makes for a suffering that is long and slow.

I guess one could say that whoever killed Ezra shared an approach I've thought of obsessively over since his murder.

I've known from the beginning he didn't do this to himself. He was too self-absorbed to have the neurological pathways to take himself out of this world.

Epilogue

Sasha
2 years ago
June 25th

Vivian said she'd left her wedding ring on the counter. I took a mental note of that. She also mentioned her keys were tucked away into her purse, so I mentally noted that, too.

These accounts tempted me as I lifted the sliding glass door at the back of the home with the help of a simple flat-headed screwdriver. Straight up and out of the track, the patio door shifted past the attempted lock and slid open, clearing the way for my entry.

I stood in the home's aroma of vanilla bean for several minutes, scanning the Bozzelli residence.

My eyes were snagged by the sharp corners of a glistening princess-cut diamond on the countertop, exactly where Vivian said her wedding ring was. Next to that was where her purse settled, also just as she willingly shared.

I took that as her blessing.

After slipping the ring into my pocket and the keys into my hand tight enough to avoid noise, I made my way to a tiresomely long staircase. Each of my steps sucked a bit of air from my lungs, leaving me faint by the time I finally reached the top.

Straight ahead at the end of the hall was the master bedroom. When I creaked the door ajar, the dramatic rusty hinges echoed, causing me to flinch, sending the keys to smack against the hardwood panels.

My pupils dilated as I strained my vision in the dark for his reaction. The knocks of my heart against my chest were as hard as a policeman's knuckles on a door to a home with a warrant.

Searching his face for alertness, I saw no signs of consciousness. My heart rate slowed to the speed of his peaceful chest, rising and falling with each drunken breath he took.

Drunk out of his mind.

He's going to sleep as hard as a rock tonight.

Vivian was right.

I walked around to the side of the bed, where he lay peacefully for now. Beside him was another set of keys, presumably his. I gathered those into my other hand and realized I was standing right above the garage when my plan puzzled into place.

I made my way to the garage at that point. I fired the engine to Vivian's car first with nearly a full tank, then Ezra's with three-fourths of a tank. I revved them both, filling the garage with gas to quicken the process.

In case that alone didn't do the job, I turned on the propane grill as high as it could go before leaving the door slightly open for gas to leak inside.

Before slipping back out through the patio door and placing it shut as it was before, I turned every burner of the gas stove to high and set the oven to broil.

Ms. Joyce and I made eye contact through the window in the kitchen. *Does she ever sleep?* I thought.

I know I told Vivian not to trust her, but I get what she meant now. It's like Ms. Joyce knew what I had done. She gave me a nod as if she approved.

Although I felt confident that this could easily be seen as suicide, I was prepared in case his death was seen for what it really was. I knew it was only a matter of time before they would suspect me since I was Vivian's ride to the airport.

With that in mind, I went to the bar and worked on inventory for several hours in order to have a time-stamped alibi because his death wouldn't take place for several more hours.

Inventory was only half of the truth, however.

I spent the other half of my time that night researching how to sell a wedding ring for the most amount possible.

Author's Note

To my readers, thank you for trusting my ability to tell a story worthy of your time. I have immense appreciation for your support of my debut.

Thank you to my family friend, Nicole Hurt, for being a critical reader and soundboard throughout the writing process.

To Brooke with *The Final Chapter Book Designs,* thank you for a book cover that exceeded my imagination!

And finally, to my friends and family who supported me with publishing my debut, THANK YOU!

Please consider leaving an Amazon and/or Goodreads review! I would so, so appreciate you sharing your thoughts with fellow readers to encourage them to read my work. There is nothing like word of mouth!

About Author

D. Laray is a self-published author with a financial services/banking career. She discovered her passion for writing through her hobby as an avid reader.

Her vision is to publish several suspense, thrillers, mysteries, and domestic fiction novels. D. Laray is devoted to dreaming up stories that leave her readers with enough closure to make them feel the blues but enough openness to leave their minds wandering.

With a mission to encourage her audience to discover and reinforce their passion for reading, D. Laray writes to tug at the heartstrings of her readers and present shocking twists.

Connect with D. Laray:

Website: dlarayauthor.com
(join the VIP Reader's Club for exclusive updates!)
Email: dlarayauthor@gmail.com.
TikTok and Instagram: @dlarayauthor
Goodreads: goodreads.com/dlarayauthor
Facebook: https://www.facebook.com/dalajia.williams/

Book Club Conversation Starters

1. Who was your favorite character, and why?
2. Who was your least favorite character, and why?
3. What shocked you the most throughout the story?
4. Which scene from *I Said I Was Gone* sticks with you the most?
5. Vivian grew up in a toxic household. She never had a good relationship with her neglectful mother, and her father wasn't present. How do you think this affected her adulthood? Did it have any positive impacts on her life?
6. Sasha did a lot for Vivian, but it wasn't always legally or morally right. Would you consider Sasha to be a good friend?
7. Do you think Sasha is in the right or wrong for killing Ezra?
8. Sasha was methodical and calculated in her actions. Do you think she knew she was going to murder Ezra, or does it seem spur of the moment? If you believe it was premeditated, do you think it was her first time committing a crime like this?
9. What did you think of Lily's relationship with Tony before things got rough? Did you notice red flags before Vivian did?
10. How was Vivian's bond with Lily similar to the bond she

had with Sasha?

11. Vivian took back her high school sweetheart, James Pierce. Do you think she should have?
12. Vivian never ended up forgiving her mother. Should she have? Do you think she will in the future?
13. What did you learn from *"I Said I Was Gone"* by D. Laray?

Made in the USA
Las Vegas, NV
22 January 2024

84758015R00104